To Everyone

e Primary

**icked
Stepmother**

Best Wishes

Karen Clayton

My Wicked Stepmother

Karen Langtree

© Karen Langtree, 2008

Published by OneWay Press, November 2008

Reprinted 2011

ISBN 978-0-9561086-0-9

Cover created by Clare Brayshaw

Prepared and printed by:
York Publishing Services Ltd
64 Hallfield Road
Layerthorpe
York YO31 7ZQ
Tel: 01904 431213
Website: www.yps-publishing.co.uk

Karen was born in Newcastle in 1969. She has always loved writing stories and songs. She studied literature and drama at college and is now a primary school teacher. She lives in York with her two children and some naughty guinea pigs!

She had her first children's musical, The Rainboat, published in 2002.

Karen loves to create. She says, 'I love seeing something emerge that was born in my imagination; it's so exciting.'

Visit her website at www.karenlangtree.com or email her at karen.langtree@btinternet.com

Acknowledgements

Thank you to my parents who always believe in me and encourage me.

Thank you to my children Rachael and Jack. Rachael helped me design the cover and gave me lots of great publicity with her friends.

Thank you to Ian who believed in me, read my stuff and pushed me to believe in myself.

And thank you Joanna, my friend who always called herself the wicked stepmother! This book would not exist without you.

Chapter One

Goodbye

You think this book is just another silly fairytale, don't you? After all, wicked stepmothers are one of the main ingredients. But this is no fairytale; this is my life. And wicked stepmothers do exist. I've got one. Her name is Eve.

It all kicked off on a Saturday in January. I was fourteen and Natalie, my sister, was seven. It was a weird day, really. That's the only way to describe it, and even calling it weird seems weird! Nat and I are early risers so we sneaked downstairs, as usual, so as not to disturb Mum and Dad. Nat switched on the TV and I went into the kitchen to get some cereal. Dad was sitting there, drinking coffee. That was the first weird thing. Mum and Dad rarely got up before ten on Saturdays. He was wearing an old T shirt and jeans. His mousy hair was sticking out like a loo brush and he had bags under his eyes.

'Having a bad-hair day, Dad? What are you doing up so early?'

He gave me this kind of watery smile and tried to laugh, except it came out like he'd gulped his coffee down the wrong way. 'All right, Lou?'

Was *I* all right? 'Yeah Dad,' I said, 'but what about you?'

He must have realised how odd it was then, him sitting there, at eight o'clock on a Saturday, looking like a scarecrow and drinking coffee. He gulped another mouthful. 'Oh, I guess this seems a bit... hmmm,' he said vaguely, glancing down at his clothes. 'I'm just waiting for your Mum and then we've ...I've got something to tell you.'

'What?'

'Erm...best wait 'til mum comes down. It involves us all.'

'Okay,' I said. Weird, I thought.

I took Nat some breakfast and we watched TV. I got into the Saturday morning show and forgot about Dad until Mum appeared at the living room door. She was dressed too. She looked tired.

'Okay girls?' she said, on her way to the kitchen.

'U-huh,' was the reply from both of us. Nat didn't even look up from the TV. But I was curious by this time. Both parents were out of bed. It was only eight thirty.

'Don't you think that's weird, Nat?' She didn't reply. 'Nat!' I insisted, shoving her in the back.

'Hey! Get off.' She swiped an arm in my direction.

'Nat, Mum and Dad are up. Something's going on.'

'What? I'm trying to watch this,' she scowled, turning the TV up.

Mum came back. 'Girls, turn the TV off will you, your Dad and I need to tell you something.' She headed back to the kitchen.

'Come on,' I said, flicking the off button and virtually dragging Nat behind me.

I wanted to know what was going on. I must admit, I already had a bad feeling. You know when you feel like there are gremlins in your stomach pinching your insides then laughing about it? I thought perhaps they were going to tell us that Dad had lost his job, or we weren't going on holiday this year, or even that someone was really sick. I never dreamt what it was they were actually going to say.

Nat and I stood in the kitchen doorway, leaning on the doorposts. Mum stood propped against the work surface and Dad was still sitting where I'd found him when I first came into the kitchen. There was this awkward silence as we looked at each other warily. Mum glared at Dad. He never looked at her, so he didn't get the vibes she was sending him.

'Well Mike,' she snapped, 'It's your call, are you going to speak?'

Dad rubbed his hand across his face. Then he simply blurted it out.

'I'm leaving.'

He looked at me and Nat like a frightened little boy.

'Leaving where Dad?' asked Nat. 'Are you getting a new job or something?'

The gremlins suddenly started jumping up and down and I thought I was going to be sick. I wanted to tell Nat not to be so silly: that he was leaving us of course. He was splitting up with Mum. But, I couldn't speak. Dad also seemed paralysed. Suddenly he began to sob and buried his face in his hands. We'd never seen Dad cry before. I still couldn't move, but Nat ran over to him and put her arms round his shoulders.

'Daddy, what's wrong? …Why are you crying?'

'Oh sensitively handled, Mike! Well done!' Was all Mum could say. She prised Nat from Dad's shoulders and sat down opposite him, with Nat on her knee. I pulled off some sheets of kitchen roll and gave them to Dad who was now wiping his nose with the back of his hand. I also sat down.

He began to try and explain. 'I'm so sorry girls. I'm not doing this very well.' He blew his nose. 'I am not going to be living with you and Mum any more. I'm moving out this morning. Your Mum and I have had a long talk about this and it's for the best. You see, I ….I've met someone else… another lady… who I … I want to live with now and your Mum and I …well we don't love each other like we used to. But we love you both as much as ever; I want you to know that more than anything else. I'm still very fond of your Mum because, well, she gave me you two and we've had lots

4

of good times together. But...now I can't stay here any more. I'll still be able to see you lots, I just won't live here anymore. I'll still be your Dad. And I'll love you just as much as ever.'

Finally, he finished rambling. Mum scowled at him. I stared at him but tears were silently running down my face. I could taste them. Nat was crying too, but she had lots of questions.

'Why don't you want to live with us anymore Dad? And what's wrong with Mum? She's nice. You do love her. You married her so you must love her...'

'I'm so sorry love, it's hard to explain to you, but Mum and I are not going to stay together.'

'Are you going to get a divorce?' I asked quietly.

'Well, yes, I think we will eventually Lou,' he replied, squeezing my hand.

Mum decided it was time to explain some practical things to us. 'Your Dad is going to live across the other side of town in Queen Elizabeth Road, near Jubilee Park. We've agreed for now that you will go and stay with him for one day and night at the weekends. We've got his phone number so you can ring him if you want to talk to him anytime. Now, I think you should go Mike, so the girls and I can get our heads sorted out.' Mum didn't even look at him; she just waved her hand in the direction of the door.

'Yes, sorry. Right. I'll ring you tonight to see if you're okay girls.' He stood up and kissed and hugged us both for a very long time. I felt so sick. I wanted to speak but I couldn't. I put my hand to my throat as if to try and release the words. Nat clung to Dad, burying her face in his T shirt, sobbing. Dad was sniffing and wiping his face with his hand. Mum pulled Nat away from him.

'Just go!' she snapped.

'Daddy!' Natalie wailed reaching for him.

He hurried up the stairs to get his things.

I looked at Mum with Nat on her knee, clinging to her. Mum was stroking her hair and staring at nothing. Nat kept catching her breath as her sobs gradually got further and further apart, until they stopped. I just felt numb, I guess. No one spoke for what seemed like forever.

Suddenly Mum shook her head as if she had just realised how to chase the whole mess away.

'Okay,' she said, 'I know we're all feeling really awful inside right now, and kind of like.... a washing machine has just gone into spin in our stomachs. So, there's only one thing for that, McDonald's! Come on let's get dressed and go.'

'But what about Dad?' I asked. ' He's still here.'

'Oh yes, ok. We'll wait till he's gone, then we'll go.'

I wandered off in a daze to get dressed. Another weird thing. McDonald's, right now? What was Mum thinking of?

We were dressed as we said goodbye to Dad half an hour later.

'Bye then sweethearts. I'll call tomorrow,' Dad said trying to smile.

Nat clung to him, crying for him to stay, begging mum to make him stay. Mum's face was stony. She didn't even come to the door. She just sat on the stairs. I couldn't speak. Dad prised Nat from his body with my help. We watched him drive off. My face was tear-streaked. Nat just sobbed 'Daddy, Daddy' over and over again. Mum began to cry as I closed the door.

'Sorry,' she whispered. We just hugged her until she stopped. We needed to be strong for her just then; even little Nat stopped crying.

At McDonald's Nat had a Happy Meal, I had cheeseburger and fries and Mum just had fries. She sat and sucked each one for ages before she swallowed it. The toys in the Happy Meal were promoting the latest Disney film and normally Nat was excited to see what she'd got. But today she wasn't bothered about it and it didn't do much anyway. There were lots of families around us having a good time. I noticed a few children with just their dads and wondered if they were visiting them for the weekend. They didn't look as happy to me as the children with both parents.

'Mum, will we have to move house?' Nat asked.

'No love, your dad will have to make sure we can stay there.'

'Will I still be able to go to Brownies on Fridays? Dad usually takes me.' Nat said.

'Yes, love. We'll work something out, don't worry.'

There was a pause. 'Will we still have the same last name as dad?'

'Yes Natalie, of course you will,' Mum bristled.

Another pause. Then I said, 'Who is this woman dad's met? When will we have to meet her?'

'Oh I don't know. Some floozy. She's called Eve or Evie or something like that. Can we drop it now?'

We didn't say much after that for a long time.

'So, how are you getting on with that Science project Lou?' Mum said suddenly.

'Okay,' I replied. Pause. We slurped our drinks.

'Nat, do you want to have Katie round for tea this week?' Mum asked.

'No thanks,' Nat answered. Another pause and more slurping.

'Well, what shall we do tomorrow?' Mum said. 'How about the cinema?'

We looked at each other then shook our heads. Mum reverted to silent staring.

After McDonald's Mum said, 'Let's go shopping.' So we trailed round lots of clothes shops. We did get some very nice tops and Nat got some expensive trainers. Mum said I could have some too but I didn't really want any. Mum bought herself a new bag. It was dinky and sparkly; the kind you might take if you're going out for the evening. But none of us were particularly excited like we normally would be.

Then we went to Pizza Hut for tea, even though it was only 4 o'clock. We sat in there for what seemed like hours, getting refills of coke and lemonade.

'Can we go now, Mum?' asked Nat.

'Yes love, where shall we go now?' she said trying to muster some enthusiasm.

'Home, please,' Nat replied.

'Oh,' sighed Mum. 'Yes, of course. Is that the time, we've been out for ages, haven't we?'

'Come on Mum,' I said, 'it'll be all right.'

She smiled weakly at me. 'Of course it will love. Come on then.'

Chapter Two

Let me introduce you

All day Sunday Mum had been on another planet. She had cooked, ironed and talked on auto pilot. Nat had spent the day watching DVDs and asking if she could ring Dad. He had rung on Saturday night but Mum would not let her ring him now. Nat got cross with Mum and refused to speak to her so I had to relay messages between them. I got annoyed with the two of them so in the afternoon I retreated to my room and read what I had written last night in my diary.

Today Dad left us. How about that? Nothing unusual there then! Happens all the time to people. So why do I feel so bad? How could he be so selfish? He's putting some woman before us. Eve or something, she's called. He can't really love us if he can put his love life first. I hate him. I don't ever want to see him again.

At that point I had slammed my diary shut and cried into my pillow so no one could hear me. As I read it again I added today's thoughts.

Actually, I don't hate him if I'm honest. I just can't get my head round what he's done. I still love him. He's my Dad. But the whole thing stinks. Nat is so upset. Mum is behaving weirdly. It's all gone wrong. I hate IT!

On Monday we went to school as normal, except of course it wasn't 'as normal.' Mum came with us to speak to Nat's head teacher and my form tutor about our 'situation' as she called it. First we called at Greenfield Primary. I stayed in the car while Mum went in with Nat. It seemed to take ages. I was getting fidgety. Eventually she took me on to St. Aidan's Comprehensive. I felt really self-conscious going in with my Mum. Once my form tutor knew about the 'situation' she was extra nice to me for the rest of the week. She told me I could talk to her any time. And she said if I found it difficult to concentrate on homework, not to worry about it. Tempting!

At break I told my best friend Zoe what had happened. She wasn't shocked or anything because she's lived with her Mum and her Mum's boyfriend since she was five. Her Dad left them for another woman and she doesn't see much of him now. I had loads of questions for her.

'Did you see your Dad much at the start?'

'Yeah! I think so,' she mused. 'It seems ages ago now.'

'Don't you miss him?'

'Nah, not really. He just messes things up when he turns up to see me, once in a while. He never let's Mum know, he just comes round one weekend and demands that I drop everything and go to his house. Well I don't need that kind of hassle in my life!'

I had this picture of Zoe's Mum standing there with her hands on her hips, shouting that at Zoe's Dad.

'Anyway I get on much better with Rick, he's a real laugh.' Rick was her mum's boyfriend.

'Isn't your Dad living with someone?'

'Yeah! That woman! I can't stand her. '(There was Zoe's Mum again!) 'She once came round our house with my Dad and shouted some really awful things at Mum. She was calling her 'effing' this and 'effing' that. Cow! Mum was in tears. Rick came in and chucked them out. He nearly punched my Dad but Mum grabbed his arm. She was going 'he's not worth it Rick, don't hit him. He'll get you locked up.' When they'd gone she said I was never 'effing' going to Dad's again while that woman was around.'

'And have you never been since?'

'Yeah! After a few months Mum gave in and let me go next time Dad came barging in. He said if she didn't, he'd get the CSA on her and that fathers have rights too.'

By the end of the week, and lots of talking to Zoe, my head was spinning with worries about what was going to happen now. I never mentioned any of this to

Mum of course, because that would only worry her. I decided just to write it all in my diary. I don't know why, but it made me feel better to be able to sort of tell someone.

Today at school Zoe told me all about her dad and his girlfriend. She really hates her and her dad sounds like a loser. I hope my dad won't turn into one but what if he does? He might stop wanting to see us? He has phoned every night this week, but maybe that's just out of guilt or some kind of early effort to keep in touch which will fade away til he never rings anymore. And then there's this woman that Dad has 'shacked up with' as Zoe calls it. Will she rant on at Mum and try to stop Dad seeing us? It's scary to think about it. I don't want to not see Dad anymore even if I do hate what he's done to us.

Friday night came and Dad still wanted to see us. Nat and I packed a little bag of clothes and things to go and stay at Dad's on Saturday. It felt really strange. Mum was acting very cheery; chatting about how it would be nice for us to stay with Dad and how he'd probably spoil us rotten. That's what weekend Dads are supposed to do, apparently.

'Will that woman be there?' Nat asked all of a sudden.

'Do you mean Dad's girlfriend?' said Mum, almost spitting out the last word. 'I expect so, after all it's her house he's living in.' Mum's mood changed after that. She was quiet but when either of us asked even a simple question she snapped at us. We certainly didn't ask about the girlfriend any more.

Saturday morning came. Nine o'clock, on the dot, there was Dad ringing the bell.

'Dad's here,' shouted Nat, who had been looking out of the window for the last ten minutes. She rushed to open the door. 'Dad!' she shouted as he bent down and scooped her up.

'Hello my little Scatty Natty,' he grinned giving her a big kiss. 'I've missed you.'

'Hi Dad,' I said, studying my shoes.

'Hi Lou. How have you been?' He tried to kiss me. I moved.

Stupid question, I thought. 'Okay,' I said.

Mum came up behind us.

'Hi,' Dad said, apologetically. 'How are you?'

Mum chose not to answer the question, but said, 'They've got everything they'll need. I want them back by ten tomorrow morning.'

'Sure, 'said Dad, 'that'll be fine. Right then, shall we go girls?'

We said goodbye to Mum very solemnly. Mum was pretending to be very cool about it, but I did worry about her when we were riding in Dad's car. I wondered if she cried when we'd gone.

In the car Dad was asking us loads of questions about school and what we'd been doing all week. He didn't mention Mum though, so I thought it best to keep off the subject too. As we neared Queen Elizabeth Road Dad got a little more nervous.

'You're going to meet someone new this morning.'

Obviously, I thought!

'You'll really like her when you get to know her. I know she won't be a patch on your Mum, and she's not meant to be the same as Mum, but just give her a chance and be nice to her, eh?' Dad stammered on nervously. 'She's really fun to be with and she really likes children.'

'Does she have any children?' I asked, abruptly.

'No, not yet,' Dad said. 'She's a bit younger than me.'

'Are you and her going to have a baby one day then Dad?' I asked, much to Dad's surprise.

'Well, we might, but not for a long time.'

'You'd have to get married first, wouldn't you Dad?' said Nat as if she knew all about these things.

'No, they wouldn't,' I snapped, knowing much more about these things! 'You can have kids any time. But you're not going to are you Dad?'

'No, no, we're not. Let's take things slowly. Just meet her and see if you like her. And please, be nice to her, okay?'

'Okay Dad,' we agreed.

We were just pulling up outside the house. Number 112 Queen Elizabeth Road was a small terraced house with one window downstairs next to the door and two windows above. I wondered if there would be enough room for us all. My stomach was doing somersaults now. All the nasty words about Zoe's dad's girlfriend burbled round in my brain. Nat was fidgety too, looking up at the house with big saucer eyes.

As Dad was getting our stuff out of the boot, Nat whispered to me, 'Do we have to stay here tonight?'

I squeezed her hand. 'It'll be alright,' I smiled, trying to convince myself as much as Nat.

Dad bent into the car. 'Ready?' he grinned.

I smiled my best plastic smile and pushed Nat gently in the back. 'Yep!'

As we walked through the door I could hear pop music playing in the kitchen. The hall was quite dark and narrow.

'Hi love, we're home,' Dad shouted along the hall.

Love? Home? Whoa! That didn't seem right. Before I realised I'd said anything, the words came out. 'We're *not* home, actually Dad. This is *not* our home.' I bit my tongue, I hadn't meant for that to happen.

'No, sorry you're quite right,' he agreed. 'I'm home. But one day I hope you'll think of this as a second home.' He smiled a pathetic smile.

'Sorry,' I said.

'It doesn't matter.'

'Hi sweetheart,' came a voice from the kitchen. Then she appeared sweeping up the passageway in a long, hippyish skirt and white clingy top. She kissed Dad, on the lips, (not like Mum did) then she said, 'Hello Natalie, Louise, It's good to meet you at last.'

Nat and I did a sort of smile. The kind where your mouth turns up a bit but your eyes don't take part. I managed a 'Hi.' Nat didn't speak.

'Let's go into the lounge,' Dad suggested and led the way.

It was small, but light flooded in from the back window and made the room feel cosy and cheerful. The walls were painted in a gentle cream colour. There was a large, black and white drawing, in a chunky wooden frame, above the fireplace, of a girl looking wistfully at a daisy chain she was making. On the mantelpiece were three photos: One of me, one of Nat and, in between them, one of Dad and *her* eating ice creams somewhere last summer. Last summer, when we had all gone to Spain and he had laughed and eaten ice creams with *us*! I glowered at him. We sat down on the sofa. Dad stood in front of the fireplace and she sat in the armchair.

There was just a fraction of an awkward silence as they smiled at us and we waited.

Dad cleared his throat then, gesturing towards her, he announced, 'Louise, Natalie, let me introduce you to Eve.' He made it sound like he was introducing us to the queen!

Eve jumped up out of her seat and knelt down in front of the sofa. 'I *am* very pleased to meet you,' she said, smiling and taking a hand each in hers. Whoa! Again, before I could stop myself, I pulled my hand away. Her smile wobbled just a little. She jumped up and, as breezily as she could, said, 'Right who'd like a drink and some cake? I've made some apple cake this morning.'

'Thanks,' I said, trying to make up for the hand thing.

'Good, won't be a tick.' She swished back into the kitchen. Dad smiled at us, encouragingly.

'She's nice, isn't she? Once you get to know her a bit, you'll really like her.'

I nodded and smiled, but deep down, I didn't intend to get to know her.

Chapter Three

Fairground Fiasco

While we were politely eating apple cake (which, I admit, was good) Dad told us that he and Eve had planned a trip to the fair this afternoon. Every year a huge fairground came and parked up in the fields on the outskirts of town. We'd gone the last few years with Mum and Dad and had a great time. I wondered if Mum would mind us going without her. Dad was telling Eve how I'd thrown up on the waltzer last year. He even told her the embarrassing ghost train story from years ago, when I hid in the bottom of the car and wouldn't come out until I saw daylight. They were all laughing at that, except me. (I was probably scowling at Dad!) Eve quickly suggested we tell some embarrassing stories about Dad instead. When Nat and I didn't volunteer any, she told us how she and Dad had been decorating the kitchen a few weeks ago.

'This little teeny weenie spider landed on your Dad's face and he jumped around and screeched like a tarantula was attacking him! I had to rescue him and the spider! Then I had to calm him down with a cup of tea.'

Dad went bright red and for the first time I found myself genuinely smiling. As I looked at Nat she was giggling behind her hands. My smile grew wider.

After lunch we set off to the fair. Nat and I sat quietly in the back of the car.

'So,' said Dad, in his Mr. Jolly voice, 'This is nice isn't it? Off to the fair. Wonder what we'll do first?'

No reply from the back.

'I bet Nat will want me to win her a coconut eh?' he chortled. 'Remember how awful I am at that Nat?'

Nat gave a faint smile.

'Oh and I'll have to have a go on the hammer thing,' he said.

Eve joined in. 'I bet he can't even get it to shoot up half way can he girls?'

No answer from the back.

'Cheek!' said Dad, 'I once got it right to the top.'

Eve persisted. 'Do you like the dodgems?'

'I do,' Nat piped up. I frowned at her.

'What about you Louise?'

'No.'

'Ah well, never mind. What is your favourite ride?'

'Haven't got one,' I said.

'Oh ok.'

I stared out of the window. Eventually she shut up. Silence returned to the car.

When we got there we all walked round together looking at the stalls and rides. Nat and I did love the fair really and I found myself talking a bit more. Nat was getting excited and asking Dad which rides we could go on. Neither of us really spoke to Eve unless she spoke to us. For a start we didn't really know what to call her. No one would have expected us to call her Mum, but calling her Eve felt funny too, even though it was her name. Maybe I was imagining things, but people were giving us funny looks. There was no way Eve looked old enough to be our Mum. I thought she was about twenty. (Actually she was twenty eight.) She had black, sleek hair down to her waist and she had her nose pierced. She had two earrings in each ear and was also really slim and tanned. I could see why Dad had fallen for her looks. Poor Mum. She couldn't help it if she was old and a bit wrinkly. I made a note in my head to tell Mum that Eve was very ugly and twice Dad's age.

We went on loads of rides and bought candy floss. We played hoopla, hook a duck and camel racing. Dad managed to win a coconut. I don't know how. The closest he came to hitting anything was when he nearly knocked the stall holder's hat off. I think she gave him the coconut to get rid of him. Eve liked going on all sorts of rides. Dad persuaded me to go on the Twister with her while he took Nat on the Merry-go-round.

We squealed together and I couldn't help laughing as I was flung against her. Then Nat needed to go to the loo. Dad and I were just about to go on the Sky Flyer and didn't want to lose our place in the queue, so Eve said she'd take Nat. Nat was okay about it, so they went off to the toilets and we said we'd meet at the burger stand when we'd finished the ride.

Dad and I waited ten minutes at the burger stand. 'They're taking ages!' Dad sighed looking at his watch again. 'What on earth are they doing?'

I was wondering that myself. Nat wasn't one for hanging around when she needed the loo.

'Should we go and meet them Dad?' I asked.

'Let's give them five more minutes. Maybe they're on their way here and we might miss them if we go wandering off.'

So we waited but still they didn't come. I was starting to get butterflies in my stomach again and horrid thoughts started to flit across my mind. What if Eve was really a child kidnapper and she'd just been waiting for the chance to abduct one of us? After all, she'd said she was *very* pleased to meet us. I looked at Dad. I'm sure he was looking worried too. His forehead was wrinkling and his mouth was all scrunched up.

'Let's go and see where they are,' he decided. We walked, rather quickly, over to the toilets. 'You go in and see if they're still there.'

They weren't. So we walked, even more quickly,

back to the burger van. No sign of them.

'Oh, you know what?' said Dad, feigning a smile. 'There's another burger van over the other side of the field. They've probably gone to the wrong one. I bet they're standing wondering where *we've* got to. Come on.'

We marched over to the other van. They weren't there. Now it wasn't butterflies in my stomach but frogs doing great leaps. I felt a bit sick. How would we break the news to Mum that Nat had been abducted? Dad started rubbing his eyebrow like he always did when he was worried or thinking hard.

'What do you think has happened Dad?' I asked tentatively, not really wanting him to confirm my fears.

'Oh they're probably wandering round the fairground looking for us, just like we're looking for them. Come on, all we can do is keep searching.'

'Has Eve got a mobile Dad? You could call her.'

'No, love, she doesn't carry one. Thinks they're an intrusion on your freedom or something. But it would be really handy right now. Bit of a pain this. Sorry it's spoiling your fun.'

Spoiling my fun! Is that what he thought I was thinking? 'Dad, I'm not bothered about my fun, I'm just worried about Nat.'

Yes, sorry love, of course. So am I, but I'm sure she's safe with Eve. They're just a bit lost, that's all.'

Then I saw Eve walking over by the hoop-la: Alone. I was relieved and terrified all at once. Relieved that she couldn't have abducted Nat, but terrified that Nat must be out there somewhere by herself.

'Dad there's Eve!' I yelled, and began running towards her. We were both shouting her name.

'Oh Mike,' she gasped. 'It's Nat, I've lost her. I'm so sorry. I've been looking everywhere for her and for you. I've been round the whole field twice and I can't see her anywhere. I'm so sorry, I'm sorry.' She burst into tears and flung herself at Dad.

Dad grabbed her by the arms and held her away from him so he could look into her face.

'Right calm down, come on,' he said firmly. 'Where did you last see her?'

She gulped and tried to compose herself. 'She was in the toilets. I let her go in by herself, she wanted to, and I waited outside. Then I saw this sweet stall and thought it would be nice to get the girls some sweets, so I shouted in the door where I was going and I'd be back in a minute. When I came back she was gone. I looked in every cubicle, everywhere. She'd gone. I'm so stupid, I'm sorry.' She started to blub again.

'Too right!' I burst out, 'How stupid is that to leave a seven year old kid alone at a fairground.' I sounded just like Mum. 'I shouldn't have let her go off with YOU! We don't even know you!'

'Louise!' Dad exclaimed.

'What? It's all your fault. Nat has probably been abducted and it's all because you've gone off with HER!'

'Enough!' Dad shouted. He shocked me. I shut up.

'Now lets all calm down. We'll only find her if we think clearly and work together. Is there an information point or something here? We could see if they could make an announcement. Where else would she have gone?'

'Should we split up Mike? I could go one way and meet you somewhere?' Eve suggested.

'Dad, you can't trust her. What might she do when she finds Nat?' All my frightening thoughts were about to pour out of my mouth. Eve looked horrified and about to cry again.

'What? You're not helping, Lou. Yes, I think that would be a good idea,' he nodded to Eve. 'We'll meet you back here in ten minutes, okay?'

She nodded, biting her lip, and hurried away. Dad and I went in the opposite direction. We searched everywhere we could think of. We didn't see an information point. There were so many people, it was hopeless. Dad was frantically asking people if they'd seen Nat, describing her to them: Small, shoulder length brown hair, freckles, brown eyes, red jumper and jeans. They'd shake their heads and promise to keep an eye out for her. After ten minutes we went back to meet Eve. She was alone. Dad was trying to keep calm.

'I think I'd better go back to the car. My phone's in there. I'd better call the police. I don't know what else to do. She's been missing for nearly an hour.'

'Do you want us to keep looking, Mike?'

'Yes, you go round the ground again and meet me back at the car.' He meant both of us. If he thought I was going with her, he was wrong.

'I'm coming with you Dad.'

'Oh. Yeah, okay, Lou.' I saw him shoot an apologetic glance at Eve. After what she'd just done! Dad and I hurried back towards the car.

'Do you think she could have been abducted, Dad?' I asked.

He stopped abruptly and as I looked into his face I knew he did. 'Oh Lou, this is such a nightmare. I really hope she's just wandering round the fairground, I'm sure she is. But, we have to act quickly because….. you never know what kind of people are about.'

We began walking again, quicker than before.

'Are you going to phone Mum?'

'No… not yet. Don't want to worry her right now. I'm sure we'll find Nat. We'll just give it a bit more time. Wait 'til I've spoken to the police.'

I did feel sorry for him (a bit). But if he hadn't left Mum none of this would have happened. Mum would have been at the fair with us, and she would never have left Nat alone in the toilets. Actually I was really angry with him. As we marched along I wanted to give him a kick in the shins. I didn't though. I decided I'd write it all down in my diary tonight instead.

However, as we came in sight of the car, a flood of joy and relief replaced my anger with Dad and Eve. Dad had seen her too.

'Natalie!' we both screamed and sprinted towards the car. She was sitting on the grass at the back of the car, with her knees tucked up to her chin. When she saw us she jumped up and started running towards us. We fell on each other in a big heap.

'Nat, oh Nat, thank goodness you're safe,' Dad gasped, almost crying.

She clung to him.

'It's okay darling. It's okay. We're here now. We're all together. You're safe.'

'It's all right Nat, we won't let you get lost ever again,' I added.

When she'd calmed down a little, Dad picked her up and carried her to the car. He opened it and sat her in the passenger seat.

'What happened love, and how did you get back here?'

'Well Eve was gone when I came out of the toilet so I didn't know what to do.'

'She said she'd told you where she was going,' I interrupted.

'She didn't,' said Nat.

'I knew she was lying,' I hissed.

'Maybe you didn't hear her darling. She said she shouted in to you,' suggested Dad.

'She didn't: ... Well I didn't hear her, it was quite noisy.'

'So what did you do?' Dad prompted.

'Well I thought I'd come and find you, and I

couldn't, so I walked around looking for you and I still couldn't find you.'

'Didn't anyone stop you and ask where your Mummy and Daddy were?' asked Dad.

'A man did, but I said I wasn't with my Mummy and Daddy just my Daddy, and he wanted me to go with him to find you, but I said I didn't go with strangers and I ran off.'

'Well that was very sensible, wasn't it Dad?' I said patting Nat on the shoulder.

'I guess so. Then what did you do?'

'I cried a bit behind a tent because I was frightened Dad.'

'I know sweetheart, but you were very brave really. How did you get to the car?'

'Well I remembered on a cartoon once this little boy had got lost and his Mum had told him if he got lost to go back to the car and wait, so I did that. I had to look really hard to find our car, but I saw my coat and Lou's coat in the back so I knew this was ours.'

Dad smiled with great relief and hugged Nat tight. 'You are an amazing girl. Thank God you're alright.'

'Yeah, well done Nat, I don't think I would have thought of that.'

'Right, we'll just wait for Eve, then we'll go back home. She'll be so relieved to see you, she was really worried. She'd gone to get you some sweets. Not a great idea, but she was just trying to be nice. So please, Louise, don't give her a hard time.'

I just made a humpfing noise and shrugged my shoulders.

'She shouldn't have left me Daddy. Mummy will be cross,' said Nat, innocently.

'Yes, you're right, love, she shouldn't, and Mummy *will* be cross.' Dad frowned.

'Are you going to tell her?' I asked.

'Of course, I am. She'd find out from you two if I didn't and then she'd never forgive me.' Then he mumbled, 'She probably won't anyway!'

At that point Eve came rushing over. She'd seen the three of us by the car so she was full of, 'Oh Natalie, thank God you're safe, I'm so relieved, I'm so sorry' etc.

Nat said, 'Its okay, you made a BIG mistake, but I'm okay now.'

'Oh that's very sweet of you, Natalie. You're a lovely little girl,' Eve said bending down and taking Nat's hand.

I couldn't help smirking to myself as Nat added, 'My Mummy is going to be ever so cross though.' Eve bit her lip and glanced at Dad.

'Yes, well, we'll face that one tomorrow,' Dad said. 'Right, let's go. I'm looking forward to a nice quiet evening in front of some mindless Saturday night TV.'

We got into the car and drove back to Dad's. When we arrived at the front door Nat burst into tears. 'I want to go home,' she wailed. 'I want Mum. I don't want to stay here.'

Dad and Eve tried to calm her down but nothing would persuade her to stay. They did manage to coax her into the house to have some tea, but only because Dad promised to take us straight home afterwards.

As we got into the car to go home, Eve apologised again. 'I'm so sorry, girls. This has been an awful day for you. Next time will be great, I promise.' She waved as we drove off. I deliberately ignored her and Nat wasn't looking.

Next time! I didn't see there being a next time if Mum had anything to do with it.

Chapter Four

Fireworks, Friends and Fairytales

I was right.

'Next time!' she screeched at Dad, as he tried to explain and apologise again. 'You don't think for one minute that that woman is going to be left in charge of my girls again do you?'

'She wasn't left in charge,' Dad protested.

'Exactly right! You were supposed to be looking after them. You! Their father. Anything could have happened, anything!' she screamed at him. Mum was bright red in the face.

'But it didn't! Children get lost all the time. Remember when you lost Lou at the seaside when she was only eighteen months?'

Nat and I sat quietly on the sofa, watching. We'd never seen Mum and Dad like this before.

'It was only five minutes, and I thought *you* had taken her to the shop.'

'Yes, well, everything's my fault in the end, isn't it? You never take the blame,' Dad said.

'Only because it usually *is* your fault! Anyway, she's got no idea how to look after children, that's obvious. I can't trust her, or you!'

Dad slumped down into a chair. He leant forward, resting his elbows on his knees, and sank his head into his hands. No one spoke for ages. Mum stared at him, waiting for him to take his turn in the slanging match. But he didn't say anything. Nat cuddled in to me. I couldn't move. Then slowly, Dad looked up.

'What a mess,' he said, each word preceded by a pause. Mum did not start ranting again. She waited for him to have another turn. 'I'm sorry. I don't know what else to say.' There was a long pause. I tried to think of something to say to fill it, but I couldn't. Nat's eyes darted from Mum to Dad and she kept squeezing my arm. Then Dad said, 'Do you want me to come back?'

Nat and I looked at each other. Dad was going to come back. He was going to leave that Eve woman and come home where he belonged. But then Mum spoilt it. She started ranting again.

'Oh yes, that would be just great. You'd come back here and be miserable. All you'd think about was that woman all the time. Then you'd start seeing her again and nothing would change. What do you think that would do to the girls? No way, Mike. The damage is done. I don't want you back. I want to start rebuilding our lives. I couldn't possibly just start all over again after what you've done. I want a divorce and I mean to start the process off immediately.'

Nat and I were right there and yet they were carrying on as if we were invisible. Nat's face crumpled, she began to cry and ran out of the room.

'Well thank you very much!' I shouted, and stormed after her.

Both Mum and Dad must have been stunned because they stood very still, saying nothing. I found Nat in her bedroom, sobbing into her pillow.

'Come here.' I held her.

'I hate them. I hate them both,' she cried.

'I know. They're stupid, selfish idiots. They've ruined everything!' I snarled.

The next thing we heard was the front door closing and Dad's car driving away.

Mum came up. She tried to console us and explain things to us. She tried to cuddle Nat but Nat pushed her away and clung to me.

'Leave us alone Mum,' I said, quietly.

She went to her room.

Later, when Nat was asleep and I was in bed, I updated my diary.

Today was a great success! Not! Dad's girlfriend is an idiot. She lost Nat at the fairground. Dad thinks she's so cool and he never even got angry with her about losing Nat. He got angry with me for being annoyed with her! And she's so young anyway. Not much older than me I reckon. And she's got her nose pierced. Dad would go ape if I did that! It's disgusting, my dad going off with her. He's too old. She's dead attractive, though I hate to say it, so what does she see in him? Then tonight he offers to come back home and Mum tells him to get lost. What is Mum on? Everything could be back to normal, well sort of. But no, she's too selfish as well. Too proud to take him back. They just don't think about us. Right now I feel like leaving!!

Over the next few weeks we tried to get on with a normal life, whatever that is. However, we knew that Mum had filed for divorce and Dad had not tried to stop her. Nat was really upset about it. She cried a lot in her room, especially at bed-time. She clung to Mum and begged her to persuade Dad to come home. Mum cuddled her and tried to help her get used to the idea that Dad was not coming back.

At school I kept Zoe informed of all that was going on. She'd got well into the fairground story and her theory was that my Dad had blown it big time.

'My Mum would have gone off on one!' she said. 'And that Eve woman sounds a bit dodgy if you ask me. I mean what adult in their right mind would leave a little kid alone in the loos at the fair!'

'I know,' I agreed. 'There's something not right about her. She tried to be really pally with us but that was just a front. I think she's trying to scare us off so we don't want to go and see Dad anymore.'

'Or it could be so your Mum won't let you go,' suggested Zoe.

Mum had stopped us from going to Dad and Eve's house. She had said that he could see us on a Saturday but under no circumstances could he take us back to their house or let Eve have any contact with us. Dad was really disappointed about this at first and then he got angry. I overheard several heated conversations about being reasonable and needing to build a good relationship for the future. One Saturday evening in particular sticks in my mind. Dad had just brought us back from a day out. He'd said he wanted to discuss some things with Mum, so I took Nat into the living room to watch TV. Nat got watching some game show but I listened at the door in case they said anything I needed to hear.

Dad was saying, 'The divorce will be held up you know Linda, if you make it difficult for Eve and I to have the girls regularly.'

'Well what do you expect me to do, Mike? I can't trust the woman. The first time they go to your house she nearly loses my daughter. She's irresponsible, to say the least.'

'It was an accident. For goodness sake woman can't you let it drop? Give her the chance to prove to you that she can look after the girls perfectly well. She's not forgiven herself for what happened and she just wants to put things right.'

'Maybe that's what you want, but I'm not so sure about her. She's young and gorgeous from what I gather, so I can't think she'd want two little kids spoiling your cosy, little love nest!'

Mum was beginning to get worked up. And, she must have been looking at my diary, because I'd told her Eve was about fifty, fat and ugly!

Dad started raising his voice now. 'Well yes she is young and gorgeous if you must know, but she's also intelligent and caring and she likes my kids.' Then there was a short pause and Dad's voice became calmer again. 'Look, she says she'd like to come and talk to you. She wants you to hear from her own lips how sorry she is and to ask for a second chance.'

Mum laughed, but it was more of a cackle really. 'No way! I'm not letting that woman into my house. I never want to set eyes on her if I don't have to. And she's not having access to the girls. She's crazy and incompetent!'

'You're insane,' shouted Dad. 'She's making an effort and you won't even let her try.'

'I just want my girls to be safe!' Mum shouted back.

'No,' replied Dad, 'you just can't stand to see me happy, and you can't stand the thought that the girls might like her. After all, one day, she will be their stepmother whether you like it or not and you can't stop her seeing them forever.'

'Their stepmother! Their wicked stepmother, more like. She's already tried to lose one of them! And I *can* stop her seeing them, you just watch me!'

'Don't be like this,' Dad pleaded.

'What? It's you who wants to take my children to live with some witch.'

'Oh you're being ridiculous Linda! I'll call you when you've calmed down. We've got to sort this out. It's not doing the girls any good.'

'And whose fault is that!' Mum shouted as Dad stormed out of the kitchen. I retreated into the living room so he didn't see me as he slammed out of the front door.

I sat on the sofa, staring at the TV. This man and woman were dressing up as pantomime characters and trying to act out a scene from a show. Then they got marks out of ten. The audience, and Nat, were laughing at them as they messed up the lines and kept standing in the wrong place or tripping over their costumes. Was this meant to be funny?

I walked into the kitchen. Mum was sitting at the kitchen table.

'Mum have you been reading my diary?' I asked, arms folded across my chest.

She looked up. Her eyes were red and watery. 'What?' she said, as if she hadn't understood a simple question.

'Have you been reading my diary?' I asked again. 'It's just that you said you knew Eve was young and gorgeous, when I told you she was old and ugly.'

Mum groaned. 'Oh you heard us. Sorry. We were being loud, weren't we? Did Natalie hear?'

'No, she's mesmerised by some stupid game show on TV. Have you though Mum?' She still hadn't answered my question.

'What? Oh, no love. I didn't even realise you kept a diary.'

'Well how did you know about Eve then?'

She smiled. 'Oh come on Lou. You were so over the top when you described her that I guessed you were telling me the opposite of what she was really like. And besides I know your Dad quite well and he would only go for young and gorgeous. I was young and quite pretty once myself you know.'

'You still are Mum, pretty I mean, not young, obviously.'

She suddenly burst out laughing. Then she came over and hugged me. I realised what I'd just said and I started laughing too.

'Oops! Sorry Mum.' We sat down again. 'Do you really think Eve's wicked and crazy?' I asked.

'My, my, you were listening carefully weren't you? Oh, I don't know, I'm just worried, that's all, about lots of things.'

'Are you really going to go through with the divorce?' I asked.

'Yes, Lou, we are. I can't see any way back now. Your Dad really likes... maybe loves this Eve and I can't see us patching things up.' We sat in silence for a while.

'Yeah, I think you're right,' I mused. 'He does seem to really like her. I guess I knew he wouldn't be coming back, deep down. I think maybe we should give her a chance; try and keep the peace.'

'You do?' She sounded surprised. 'Good grief! Listen to us. We sound like best friends, having a coffee and sharing our problems. Only you're the one with all the advice.'

After that incident things seemed to get better for a while. Mum apologised to Dad, on the phone, later that week and said she'd think about us being allowed to go over to Dad and Eve's house again.

Zoe said my Mum was soft to give in so easily. We were walking back from school one day and I told her what Mum had said about Eve becoming our Wicked Stepmother. Zoe laughed, then in her most dramatic voice, she said, 'Well maybe your Mum's right. Maybe she's like the one in Babes in the Wood who tries to lose the children. Or maybe she'll be like Cinderella's Wicked Stepmother and make you slaves in her house, doing all the chores. Or worse still, maybe she'll try to kill you like Snow White! Ha, ha, ha!' She cackled like an evil witch right in my ear.

'Shut up you idiot!' I gave her a shove and we giggled together all the way home. She came to my house for tea that evening and she kept cackling quietly in my ear while we were eating. Mum kept giving her funny looks and I kept kicking her under the table.

'What's wrong with Zoe?' Nat asked.

'Oh nothing,' I said, 'she's just a bit mad.'

After tea, we went to my room to listen to CDs and discuss boys, hair, clothes and stuff.

Zoe had jet black, spiky hair. She had to spend ages every morning getting it right. She always wore loads of make up for school too. She'd been told to wash it off so many times but she always came back the next day with it. Even when she got detention it didn't put her off. In the end the school just gave up trying. She had both ears pierced twice too, but at least she only wore studs to school.

'You should do something different with your hair,' she said.

I looked in the mirror. It was a bit boring just having long, straight mousy hair.

'Dye it black. And cut it short. You could look this cool too. Go on Lou. I dare ya. Do something radical.'

I tried to imagine myself with black, punky hair; or maybe a bit Goth looking. Would it go with blue eyes? Probably.

'Yeah, maybe I will.'

'My mum would cut it for ya.'

I thought dubiously of Zoe's mum's idea of fashionable.

'Erm... don't know. Mum and Dad would go mad.'

'Oh what do you care what they think? They couldn't care less about you, could they? Just do it girl.'

I paused, looking back in the mirror, then said, 'Yeah ok. When?'

'I'll ask my mum when she can do it. Maybe next

week? You bring the dye, I'll tell my mum. She'll love doing it.'

Later, at the door as Zoe was leaving, she couldn't resist one more cackle. 'See ya Snow White. Ha, ha, ha!'

'She *is* mad,' said Nat. 'Why's she calling you Snow White?'

'Oh it's just a joke from something at school today,' I shrugged, slightly relieved that she'd gone.

Mum let us go back to Eve's house the next Saturday. Dad came to pick us up and grovelled very well to Mum. Mum took full advantage of it, making sure Dad knew exactly what she expected of him: Phone her every few hours and have us back by nine that evening (no staying over yet). Nat was a bit nervous and even asked if Mum could come, proposing we could all have a nice day out together. Dad managed to persuade her that it would be okay without Mum and we left. I was a little nervous recalling how I'd felt about Eve when we last saw her. Some of the things I'd said were coming back to haunt me.

As we pulled up to the house Eve was at the door. She had a big grin on her face like she was over the moon to see us. We stepped out of the car and she came towards us as if she was going to hug us. At the last minute she thought better of it.

'Hi Louise, Natalie. It's great to see you again. I'm so pleased you've been allowed back. Come inside. I've been making loads of sweet treats that are probably really bad for your teeth!'

'Babes in the Wood!' warned Zoe in my head. 'Shut up!' I told her.

Actually, the day went well with Dad and Eve. There were no disasters and Nat was getting on well with Eve. She seemed to have forgotten that Eve had left her alone at the fairground.

'Don't you remember what she did last time?' I whispered to Nat when Dad and Eve were in the kitchen laughing about something.

'Who?' asked Nat

'Eve, of course Dummy! At the fair.'

'When I got lost you mean?'

'Yes.'

'I remember, but it doesn't really matter. I like her. She's fun. And Dad likes her. She makes him laugh a lot.'

I screwed up my face.

Dad phoned Mum every few hours, as instructed, but we didn't go very far from the house. We played games in the house and ate Eve's goodies. She had baked fairy cakes, chocolate brownies and a trifle for after tea. Later we kicked a football around in Jubilee Park: Eve and Nat versus Dad and me. They won 2–1 and Eve ran around the field with Nat on her back, singing 'We are the champions!' Then we went back to their house and ate more food, especially sweet stuff. Maybe Eve wasn't too bad after all. Maybe all Zoe's cackling had just made me more nervous.

'Have you had a good day, Lou?' Eve asked me when we were getting ready to leave.

I hesitated. 'Yeah. It's been... okay.'

'Oh I am glad. I was so nervous about you coming. You were so mad with me last time and I don't blame you. I'd really like us to be friends.'

'Today was good,' I said. 'Thanks.'

As the car pulled away Nat wound down the window to shout 'Bye.'

'See you soon. Bye.' Eve shouted, waving like crazy.

When we got home Mum opened the door to greet us. 'Have you had a nice...' was all she managed to say before Nat threw up all over her.

Chapter Five

Shock Tactics

'What the...Come on darling, let's get you inside,' Mum said to Natalie, through gritted teeth, shooting daggers at Dad.

'I'll speak to you in the morning,' she snarled at him. 'Come on Louise.'

Before Dad could speak she'd pulled me in and slammed the door with her foot. Nat had eaten far too much sweet stuff of course and then all that racing around. After Mum had settled her in bed for the night I tried to explain and even stick up for Dad and Eve a bit.

'Idiot! What was that mad woman thinking? First she tries to lose her, then she tries to poison her!'

Snow White! warned Zoe in my head. 'Shut up,' I hissed.

'What?' said Mum. I must have hissed out loud.

'Oh, ... mucked up, I was saying, she mucked up. Eve, I mean!'

'She sure did!' agreed Mum, forcefully. 'Well he can forget about you going there again.'

'But Mum, she didn't do it on purpose,' I heard myself say in Eve's defence.

'Well whatever! She's doing a fine job of looking after you!'

Mum was in a right mood so I went to bed. I wrote my diary.

Mum is absolutely crazy mad with Dad about Nat being sick everywhere. She's being so over the top. Honestly, they're all doing my head in.

I did actually have a good day with Dad and Eve today. I do want to give it a go with Eve. Nat was right. Dad is really happy with her. I didn't realise til now how little he used to laugh and stuff at home. He's changed, sort of lightened up.

I'm going to have to work on Mum to get her to let us go back again. She knows Dad's not coming back so she better not stop us seeing him.

Nat stayed off school on Monday. She was fine really but I reckoned Mum just wanted to make it seem worse when she picked up the phone to rant at Dad. When I got to school Zoe asked me about the weekend. She couldn't stop laughing as I was telling her.

'It's not that funny Zo.'

'It is though. It's hilarious. You could make it into a Sitcom. You know, like that *My Family* thing. We'd have to make the characters really over the top. You could be the main character, especially when we get your new image. You could be the cool one who's really embarrassed by the rest of them. Your dad could be this bungling kind of idiot who keeps messing things up, your mum could be this wild harpy type of character….'

'Zoe!' Stop! You're mental. So, when can your mum do my hair?'

'Thursday. She says about half four. You gonna actually do it then?'

'Yes, course I am.'

'Never thought you'd go through with it. You still might chicken out.'

'I won't. You'll see. You can come with me to buy the stuff after school.'

'Ok. I'd love to see your mum's face when she sees it. Can I come and watch? Then again, she'd just blame me so maybe not. She's a real prude your mum. Great temper though.'

'I can't wait to see her face either. She isn't going to stop me doing this. When she finds out there will be nothing she can do.'

I was looking forward to Thursday. I told Mum I was going to Zoe's for tea after school. She said fine. She was still totally pre-occupied with fuming about Dad and Eve. Nat was well fed up when I got home from school.

'Mum's been in a right bad mood all day. She's been going round muttering about Dad and Eve. When she phoned him, I could hear her getting mad even from my room. I wanted to go to school today and she wouldn't let me.'

46

'Well, she can't stop us doing everything. She is going to get such a shock on Thursday.'

'Why?'

'Just wait and see. You'll think it's wicked.'

'Tell me. Go on. I'll be your best friend.'

'Don't be silly, Nat. I can't tell you in case you let it slip by accident. Just trust me.'

She looked a bit huffily at me. 'Well I'm going to do something too.'

'What?'

'It's a secret. You'll have to wait and see.'

'Ok,' I smiled and gave her a playful shove over her bed.

I grew more and more excited about Thursday. I kept planning my new image and imagining Mum and Dad's reactions. I was a tad nervous too, but I forced the excitement to override it.

After school on Thursday I took Zoe into town.

'Right, we need Boots or Superdrug, they sell hair colour.'

We searched the hundreds of boxes of colour all trying to allure me to use them. Honey Gold, Summer Blonde, Hazelnut Whirl, Red Corvette, Ice Shimmer, the list went on. We found the black range. I mean how can you have a black range? Black is black isn't it? After about twenty minutes of indecisiveness Zoe forced me to go for Midnight Rendez Vous.

'Right let's get back to mine,' Zoe said when we were outside the shop.

'Not yet. Got something else to do first. Come on.'

Zoe started to ask questions but I just gave her a wicked grin and kept walking. We arrived outside a shop. On the sign it said *Rod's Tattoo and Piercing Parlour*.

'You're not!' Zoe exclaimed. I raised my eyebrows at her and grinned. We went in.

I looked around at the photographs, covering the walls, advertising tattoos that you could have. There were all sorts from neat little Dolphins and hearts to huge works of art sprawling across muscled chests and arms.

'Can I help you ladies?' said a rather gorgeous looking man, wearing a vest top, his arms covered in more advertising.

I gulped. Zoe flashed him her most flirtatious smile. I swallowed hard, and trying to sound confident said, 'Yes, I'd like my ears pierced twice please. Once here,' I pulled on my ear lobe, 'and again at the top. And I'd like a silver stud in my nose please.'

He smiled at me and looked me up and down in my neat school uniform. Then he turned to Zoe and nodded knowingly. 'Your idea is it?'

'No way!' She said holding her hands up as if in surrender. 'Hey, if she wants to do it I'm behind her all the way, but it's definitely NOT my idea.'

He looked at me again. 'You sure you want all that at once? It'll be really sore.' He gestured towards my uniform. 'What's the school going to say? Bet you'll get into trouble.'

'Not just with school,' Zoe laughed.

'Look, do you want the business or not? I'll go get it done somewhere else if you don't,' I said, surprising myself.

'Ok then,' the man said. 'At least I know you'll get a professional job done if I do it myself. Come and sit down. I've got some *Hello* mags over there your friend can read.'

'Oh cool,' Zoe said leaping into the squashy leather seats in the corner.

When we stood outside the shop not too many minutes later two gold studs throbbed in each ear and my nose felt like it had been stung by a killer bee. Zoe was doing really well at not laughing and trying to be sympathetic to my pain. I think she was genuinely impressed.

'You'll look really good Lou when the redness goes down. The silver nose stud is gorgeous.'

'Thanks,' I said, trying to smile. 'Right let's get to your house.'

'Are you sure you still want to do that as well?'

'Why does everybody keep asking me if I'm sure? Yes I'm sure. Come on let's get on with it.'

Zoe's mum, Lisa, smiled and bit her lip when she saw me.

'Well, well. You certainly are going for a change of image Lou. It looks great. What are we doing with the hair then?'

'I want to go really short. Layered and a bit spiky on top (not as much as Zoe's), over my ears. No fringe except little short wispy bits. Here, like this.'

I produced a picture I'd cut out of a magazine of a model. I hadn't even shown it to Zoe. 'Do you think you can do it?'

'Of course I can,' Lisa said. 'I am a hairdresser Lou. You got to trust me.'

'I do, I do. And I'll pay you for it, when I get some more cash. Just spent most of mine.'

'Nah, it's on the house. You're my Zoe's best friend. Take it as a present, to help you through your mum and dad's divorce and all that stuff.'

'Do you think it will suit me? I don't want to just end up looking like a boy.'

She studied the picture for some moments then she studied me. ' Yeah, I think it will. You might not think so at first mind, it will be dramatic. But our Zoe will help you with some make up to suit it and you'll look fab.'

I took a deep breath. 'Do it.'

My mum was going to freak; if she recognised me that is! As I walked home from Zoe's I kept touching my bare neck. It was unfamiliar to me, being used to my long hair. I also kept catching glimpses of myself in shop windows and having to reassure myself that it actually was me! My piercings had stopped throbbing now and didn't appear so angry. I thought I looked quite cool. Zoe's mum had done a great job on my hair and Zoe had made me up and given me a look verging on Gothic: Very red lips, heavy black eye liner and dark eyeshadow. It suited me. Pity I was still in my school uniform. As I reached the door of my house I hesitated. There was no going back. I ran my tongue over my teeth, tossed my head back and entered.

'Hi Mum,' I shouted casually. No answer but I could hear her on the phone. As I entered the kitchen she had her back to me. She was just ringing off. She turned.

'Lou, it's Natalie .....' She stopped and stared.

'Oh my .....what the hell have you done!'

'I'd have thought that was obvious. What do you mean, it's Nataile?' I said.

'She's gone missing. I went up to her room about half an hour ago and she was gone. I've looked everywhere for her. I've searched the garden, I've looked in the street, I've tried the neighbours. Your dad's on his way over.'

Mum was distraught. I felt a fool. All the impact of my stuff faded into insignificance.

'She planned this,' I said, almost to myself.

'What? How do you know?'

'She told me she was planning something but that it was a secret.'

'Well why didn't you get it out of her?'

'Cos I wouldn't tell her what I was planning.'

'How childish Louise. I can't believe you've done this. I'll deal with you later. She's taken her favourite cuddly dog and her backpack and coat. I can't see anything else missing. Now think, where would she go?'

'Have you tried her school friends?'

'I was just about to.'

I'll get my bike and go look round the streets and the park.'

Mum got on the phone to all the parents she knew. I went off on my bike. I knew some of Nat's favourite places. I couldn't believe she had planned to run away. I never thought she'd be brave enough. When I got back Dad had arrived.

'Oh Mike, what are we going to do? I should call the police. I can't understand it. Not Nat.'

'We've got to concentrate on finding her then we can sort out why she's done it.'

'I think it's obvious isn't it?' Mum said, giving him a hard look.

'Let's not start throwing blame around now. It's not helpful.'

At this point Dad turned round to see me coming through the kitchen door. He gawped at me and tried to suppress a smile.

'Wow!' he said. 'That's some change of image.'

'Is that all you can say?' Mum said. 'She is in big trouble later, when we've found Nat.'

'Yes, of course,' Dad said.

Mum had not had any success with Nat's friends, although Nat had told her best friend at school that she was going to teach her mum and dad a lesson.

'There's no sign of her in any of the places I can think of. I asked a few people on the street but none of them had seen her.' I said.

'I'm going to call the police,' Dad said.

By this time several of our neighbours had come to see if they could help. They were sent out to keep searching the area. The police came within half an hour and were asking Mum and Dad lots of questions. Mum started crying. Dad kept rubbing his eyebrows as he tried to keep control and think. Nat had been missing for at least three hours now and it was quite dark outside. The police were mobilizing search parties.

Dad rang Eve to tell her he was not coming home, as he would be staying to help with the search.

'No sweetheart, I think it's best you don't come here,' I heard him say down the phone, casting a sheepish glance at Mum.

'Yeah. I'll ring as soon as there's any news. Speak later. Bye.'

Mum was being comforted by a WPC. She was telling Mum reassuring stories of runaways turning up.

'What can I do Dad?' I asked. Then I burst into tears. 'This is all my fault.'

'Don't be silly Lou. How can it be?'

'I told her I was going to do this,' I gestured to my hair and face, 'and she said she was going to do something too.'

Dad pulled a 'don't quite know what to say' face and put his arm round me. 'You can come and search with me. Go get something warm on and wipe that stuff off your face. You've got black smudges all over your cheeks.'

I ran up the stairs. 'Bring that big torch with you that your mum keeps in her bedside cabinet,' he shouted.

Chapter Six

Mum's Worst Nightmare

Minutes later we were out on the streets. Mum was left with only the WPC, as the other officers joined Dad and I in the search. We were knocking on doors and asking if we could search people's gardens, garages and outhouses. By midnight there were still no sightings of her. We went home with some of the police officers and Mum made hot drinks. Actually the WPC made the drinks as Mum was shaking too much.

I went to hug her. 'You okay Mum?' I couldn't think of what else to say.

'Of course I'm not,' she snapped pushing me away.

Dad put a hand gently on Mum's arm. 'Hey, come on Linda don't take it out on Lou.'

'Oh shut up Mike. She put the idea into Nat's head. Get out there and find her. I wish I could but they say I need to be here for when she comes home.'

Dad and I retreated to the living room. There was no

point in protesting. 'What do we do next?' I asked.

Just then the officer drinking tea in the armchair got a call to his radio. Someone had seen a girl of Nat's description getting into a car with a woman at about 10.30. It appeared suspicious because the girl was so young and seemed hesitant.

Mum was hysterical. 'Oh no. She's been abducted. This as my worst nightmare. You've got to find her; please. They'll do despicable things to her. Oh God please bring her back!' With that cry for help to the Almighty she broke down.

Dad and the WPC moved to comfort Mum. I ran into the kitchen where I paced around praying silently to the same Almighty that we'd get Nat back safely. I'd never forgive myself for this.

The police officers didn't have a registration number to check, only the colour and possible make of the car: Red, could have been a Clio or a Peugeot 206.

Dad came into the kitchen with a couple of officers. They sat down at the table. 'Make us some coffees love.' They started to ask Dad a lot of questions about Nat and what was going on in our lives at the moment. I caught a glimpse of my distorted reflection in the stainless steel kettle. I looked stupid and my nose and ears were throbbing again. I ached to know what was happening to Nat. *Please God…*

I wandered into the lounge to check on Mum. She was lying on the sofa with a blanket over her. She was clutching a handful of paper tissues and seemed to be muttering to herself. The WPC, Melanie she was called, was sitting on the arm of the sofa looking rather helpless. She smiled at me.

'You Mum is just resting,' she said in a stage whisper.

'Oh,' was all I could think to say.

'Could you get some sleep do you think?'

I stared at her shaking my head. 'Hardly!'

'Sorry, stupid suggestion,' she said.

I felt rude then. 'Would you like a coffee or something?'

'That would be lovely thanks.'

'What about Mum?' Mum was still in some sort of trance which I later realised was shock. Melanie looked at her. And shook her head.

Back in the kitchen there had been some more news. A sighting of a similar child in a petrol station on the outskirts of town buying bread and milk at midnight. The cashier told police she got back into a red Clio, definitely a Clio, but couldn't be sure if it was a man or woman driving. They were going through the CCTV footage now. Dad thought it best not to tell Mum. He looked in on her and came back rubbing his eyebrow furiously. His mobile rang.

'Hi babes.' Pause. 'No. But…' He headed upstairs and I didn't hear the rest. I slumped down in an armchair having given Melanie her coffee. Images of Nat crying in the back of a car whirled around my head. Then someone was trying to stick a big needle through her nose.

The next thing I knew was Dad gently shaking me and handing me a cup of tea. A pale light was seeping through the window.

'Have they found her Dad?' I looked across at Mum. She was asleep. Melanie had disappeared.

'No love but they traced that car. Got the registration from the CCTV. They've located the address it's registered to. It's in Leeds. So that's about twenty miles away. They're on their way there now.'

My heart pounded. I tried to sip my tea and burnt my lip. 'Should we wake Mum?'

Dad looked across at her, and ran his hand across his face. 'Not yet.'

Just then the front door burst open. 'I've found her! I've found her.' It was Eve.

Dad and I jumped. My tea went all over the carpet. Seeing Eve in Mum's house was almost more startling than what she was saying. The commotion woke Mum.

'Eve! You've found her? Where? Where is she?' Dad demanded. Mum lurched off the sofa and fell onto the floor.

'What is SHE doing here?' She croaked trying to pick herself up. I went to help her.

'It's Natalie. She's safe come and see. She's in my car, asleep.'

By this time the police officers, including Melanie, had come through from the kitchen.

'Get out of my house!' Mum shrieked at Eve. 'We're

in the middle of a crisis and I don't want you here.' She launched at Eve.

'Linda!' Dad grabbed Mum by the arms and shouted in her face. The shock hit Mum like a fist. 'Eve has found Nat. She's in the car.' Mum collapsed against Dad in a violet sob.

We all rushed out to Eve's red Clio. There was Nat, asleep under a blanket. We peered in like people observing a dangerous animal in a glass case. Then Mum was sobbing and so was I. Dad opened the car and lifted Nat out. She began to stir. She looked up and saw Dad. She put her arms round his neck and he carried her inside.

There was lots of hugging, kissing, crying all round. The police radioed that she had been found and a message came in that the Clio had been a red herring: Just a single mum out too late at night with a tired and surly child.

As Dad, Mum and I huddled round Nat, I noticed the police lead Eve out of the room. 'What has Lou done to her hair and face?' Nat said.

'Never mind that,' Mum said, half smiling half scowling. 'Why did you do it Nat? Where have you been?'

'Lou said she was going to give you two a shock so I wanted to as well.'

Mum and Dad gave me a serious stare, the kind you get when you know you're going to be grounded for weeks, have your phone confiscated and lose a month's pocket money.

'But where have you been? We've been worried sick. We thought...' Dad trailed off.

'I walked and walked and then Eve picked me up.'

'Eve picked you up?' Mum said. She turned to Dad. 'She picked Nat up in a red Clio. That was the sighting the police had. She tried to kidnap our daughter!'

'Don't be ridiculous,' Dad said. 'She found her and brought her back here. Last time I spoke to her she was out in her car searching. Said she couldn't just sit there doing nothing.'

'Rubbish. She was going to abduct her but realised she'd never get away with it.'

Mum stood up. 'Where is she? Is she still here?'

Mum headed for the door to protests from Dad and Nat. We followed. She found Eve in the kitchen being questioned by the police. 'SHE tried to kidnap my daughter. I'll bloody kill her.'

'Linda!' Dad grabbed Mum. She was insane with rage. She thrashed in his grip but a police officer got up and helped Dad.

'Get her out of my house!' Mum screeched as Melanie and another officer led her back to the lounge.

Dad put his arms round Eve who looked frightened. 'It's okay love. She's in shock. I think it's best if you go home for now. I'll be there soon. You get some sleep. You've done a fantastic thing today.' He hugged her. 'It is all right for her to go, isn't it?' He looked at the remaining officer.

'Yes. It's fine. We'll be in touch.' Eve smiled weakly at us. Nat suddenly clutched her round the waist. Eve stroked Nat's hair briefly.

Dad took Eve to her car. I watched him kiss her and she was gone. He came back into the lounge and the police officers took their leave saying they would call tomorrow. When the four of us were alone and Mum was silently holding Nat, Dad said, 'We need to talk about this but not now. Let's get some sleep. I'll come round tomorrow. Will you be okay?' He said this to me rather than Mum.

'Yes Dad,' I said responsibly. He helped me get Nat and Mum into bed then he kissed me and went back to Eve.

'It's not our fault!' I protested the next day.

Family meeting in progress. Nat had explained that she had decided to walk to Dad's house, which was several miles across town. She had got lost and didn't know what to do. Several people had tried to speak to her, including a drunk old man, but she had run away. By the time Eve had found her she'd been desperate and so glad to see a familiar face.

'It's you two who should be sorry. You are screwing up our lives. You've left us, Dad, and Mum is trying to stop us seeing you. Mum is always in a bad mood and you care more about Eve than us!'

Mum and Dad stared at the floor. For once Mum didn't start ranting at Dad.

'But Nat honey, that was such a dangerous thing to do,' said Dad.

'We were frantic,' said Mum. 'don't you know how much we love you?'

There was silence. Then Nat said, 'Mum I want to go to Dad's house.'

'What, now? You can't live with him. Absolutely not. Not with that ….'

'No!' Nat shouted, making us all jump. 'I mean I want to stay with Dad at weekends. I don't want to stop seeing him. And Eve.'

I cringed slightly. Mum winced. Dad raised his eyebrows. More silence. Everyone looked at Mum.

'I'll think about it.'

'Linda! You really can't stop them coming you know. I can get a court order and….'

'Be quiet!' Nat screeched, putting her hands over her ears. Dad did.

Mum put her arm round Nat. 'We'll work something out. Now, say goodbye to your Dad. He's just leaving. Oh and Lou you are grounded.'

'Definitely,' Dad said.

'I know that!'

Dad left. I got my diary out.

Yesterday I dyed my hair black, had it cut really short and got my ears and nose pierced. I thought it looked great. Knew Mum would have a fit but was really looking forward to seeing her face. Then Nat ran away and it didn't really matter what I'd done. (Well, except that I'm grounded!)

I just hope that Mum and Dad will start behaving better. It's like a competition to see who can get their own way the most. Me and Nat are not possessions. What about what we want? Nat told them what she wants. She's getting pretty stroppy these days. Good for her.

Wonder how long I'm grounded for?

Chapter Seven

Diamonds and Divorce

Mum and Dad grounded me for a month. They agreed on that at least! Zoe was not allowed even to ring me as Mum suspected she'd had an influence on me. I refused to rat on her. Mum wanted me to take the studs out but I convinced her they would get infected and I'd end up a mess. She wrote to the school apologizing and absolving herself of blame. She made me write too: Just as well though because I reckon it got me out of a week's detentions!

Mum took some persuading, and plenty of groveling from Dad, to give Eve yet another chance, but by next Saturday she had given in. Nat was becoming very persistent these days. Eve really liked my new image. She was a bit careful around Dad as she knew he'd agreed to ground me for it. But when he went upstairs for something she told me what she really thought.

'I love what you've done with your hair Lou. It looks great. Really sophisticated. And the piercings are great. Love the silver nose stud. I've got a couple you can have if you'd like them, for when you can take that one out. Better not get anything else pierced though eh?' We shared a conspiratorial smile.

After a couple of months of day visits Mum let us stay over one night. I was really nervous that something bad might happen, but it didn't and we were all relieved. The next week when we were allowed to stay over again, Eve asked us if we'd like to decorate the spare room; to personalise it. Dad and Eve had put bunk beds in there and we were really excited about making it ours. Mum didn't like the idea. She sulked about it for ages as Nat and I chattered on and on about what we wanted to do. She kept making snide remarks about Eve. When I told Zoe what we were thinking of doing to the room she thought it was cool.

'Aw, wicked! I'd love to paint stuff like that on my walls. Mum and Rick would never let me do it. Pity you'll have to have the Barbie stuff too though.' (Nat wanted some Barbie transfers for her contribution!)

Eve had thought it was a great idea when I suggested an under sea mural. I enjoyed art at school and had started to collect pictures of sea creatures to practice drawing them. Then Dad told me Eve was an artist. She had drawn that picture of the daisy chain girl over their fireplace. I'd never thought to ask what Eve did. I had never thought about the fact that she was a real person, with a life outside of the times we saw her. Next time we went round I asked her to show me some of her artwork. It was really amazing. There was lots of stuff from her student days as well as designs she'd submitted for publication. There were watercolours, pastels, pencil drawings, charcoal, batik. She certainly was talented. She said she was a freelance artist and had done designs for all sorts of things from greetings cards to CD covers, to patterned kitchen towels! She said she'd love to help us with the room if we wanted her to. I thought that would be cool. Nat thought so too, as long as Barbie came into it somewhere!

The next two weekends were spent decorating. We had a great time. Dad was tea boy and general dogsbody, while us girls got on with the creative stuff. When it was finished it looked ace. Dad was impressed.

'Can we take a picture to show Mum?' Nat begged. Dad and Eve looked a bit unsure. 'Please, please!'

Dad got the digital camera out and took some pictures. He printed them off on the computer so we could take them home. Nat was full of it when we got back. She thrust the photos into Mum's hand.

'Look at our new room, isn't it brilliant Mum? I stuck that picture of Barbie on the wall there and Eve helped me paint a castle around her. I painted the sea too and did some of those starfish stencils.'

Mum flicked through the pictures. She never smiled once. 'Yes, it's very nice.' I talked about it a little, but thought that I should play it down. Inside I was as bubbly as Nat about it. We'd had a brilliant time doing it and Eve had been great fun. She was also a very good teacher. She'd shown us lots of things about drawing and painting we'd never learn at school. But Mum was distant. That night I wrote in my diary;

> *Had a great time decorating the walls of our new bedroom at Dad's this weekend. When we showed Mum the pics she wasn't interested. Thought she could have been a bit nicer about our artwork. I know it's hard for her. Will try to keep off the subject of Dad and Eve as much as possible.*

I told Nat not to talk about Eve, Dad or our new room in front of Mum anymore.

'Well its not like Eve's our Mum is it?' she said. 'She's just Dad's girlfriend: Like a big sister really. And our room is great.' I gave her a look. 'But I won't talk about it in front of Mum.'

All week we both tried to be ever so nice to Mum. I kept my room tidy and offered to do some washing up twice. I even snuggled up to her on the sofa one evening.

'So what's all this in aid of?' she asked.

'What?' I replied, faking innocence.

'Being extra nice to me,' she smiled. 'I can't remember the last time I was honoured with a cuddle from my eldest daughter.'

'Don't you like it?'

'Of course I do. I just wondered what I'd done to deserve it.'

'Well…. you're just a great Mum, isn't that enough?'

She put her arm round me and squeezed me. 'I'll accept that,' she smiled and she kissed me on the top of my head like she used to do when I was little.

The next Saturday, when we saw Dad and Eve, they sat us down on the sofa, opposite the daisy chain girl, while they stood nervously together. We looked expectantly at them. It was very similar to when we first met Eve.

'Your Dad and I have something to tell you. It's good news, I think!' Eve looked at Dad. 'Go on Mike,' she smiled, nudging him with her elbow.

'We've got engaged!' he blurted out, thrusting Eve's left hand high in the air. On her finger was a beautiful engagement ring with a single diamond twinkling in the sunlight. He grinned manically at us.

We both stared open mouthed. Whoa! Engaged! But Mum and Dad weren't even divorced yet. This seemed too fast. Nat looked from Dad to Eve to me, totally bewildered. I asked the questions and made the objections.

'But how can you be engaged? You're still married to Mum.'

'Well, the divorce is nearly through now. We got the decree nisi this week, which is a posh way of telling us that it's almost finalised,' explained Dad.

Finalised. This was it. Dad and Mum, finished. Mum home alone, Dad here with Eve. No going back. Forever. Eve would be our new Stepmother. Zoe was just about to cackle in my head (a sound that had long faded from my mind), when I stopped her with another question.

'But isn't it illegal or something, before you're actually divorced? I mean what if you and Mum decide to get back together?'

I couldn't believe I was saying this. I'd known for ages that they weren't going to get back together. Dad was obviously head over heels with Eve. So why was I saying such stupid things?

'Louise, soon Mum and I are not going to be married anymore. But we are still going to be your Mum and Dad. Nothing is ever going to change that. Nothing! We'll still love you just the same and....'

Suddenly Eve bent down and took Nat's hands in hers. Big tears were rolling down Nat's face.

'Aw little Nat. I'm sorry,' she gulped. Then Eve was in tears too. Then I burst into tears, then Dad. We ended up squashed together into a big, wet ball of hug. When we'd stopped crying, Eve found a box of tissues and Dad took Nat on his knee.

'Darling, things will be good again, you'll see. You have three grown ups now, who love you very much.'

'But Daddy I want you and Mummy to be together at home. I don't want you to marry Eve,' Nat said. Then turning to Eve she added, 'I do like you Eve but I want Mummy and Daddy to be home again with me.' Dad didn't know what to say. He just cuddled her tightly into him.

I dreaded telling Mum. In fact, should I tell her? Maybe Dad didn't want her to know until the divorce was final. He should tell her really. As we were getting ready to go home the next day I asked him what he was going to do.

'Of course I'm going to tell her love. I wouldn't expect you to take that on. Goodness knows how she'll react. But maybe she'll be fine. She doesn't want me back. And she's been so good about letting you two come over for ages now.'

'Maybe I should help you Dad,' I suggested. 'She might be better if she sees I'm okay about it.'

Dad looked at me for a moment with his face all screwed up. 'And are you okay about it? I mean really okay? This is so hard for you.'

'I think I am,' I replied. 'Anyway, I'll fit in better at school now that I'm from a normal family, with a Wicked Stepmother!'

He smiled, sadly.

When we got home Dad said he had something to tell Mum. I installed Nat in front of her favourite DVD then went to the kitchen. They had waited for me and I joined them round the table feeling far too grown up. Dad broke the news as gently as he could then seemed to take a deep breath and draw back as if waiting for the barrage of abuse. Mum was silent, staring into her coffee. Dad and I just watched and waited for her to do something.

After what seemed a very long time she looked up and sighed. Her eyes were watery but she didn't cry. 'I was expecting it if I'm honest. Only I thought you'd wait until we were divorced. Why do you have to get engaged so soon? Is there more news you're waiting to tell me?' She raised her eyebrows at Dad.

'No, no, nothing like that. We just …we want to get married and I wanted to …. make it official.' He pushed his hands through his hair and sighed. 'Oh it feels wrong saying this to you.'

Mum shrugged. 'Yes, well. What's right and wrong got to do with anything? I don't really know anymore. You'd better go.'

Dad stood up. I hadn't said anything the whole time and it was as if they had forgotten I was there. So I said, 'Nat and I will be okay. I mean, we'll get used to the idea.'

They both looked at me, remembering I was there at last.

'Thanks Lou,' Dad smiled, kissing me on the cheek. Mum squeezed my hand.

When Dad left, Mum went upstairs. She stayed there for a long time. Her eyes and nose were very red when she came downstairs. Nat and I gave her a big hug. Then Nat said something which made her smile.

'You know Mummy,' she began very seriously, 'We'll always love you even though you and Dad are not married anymore. You'll always be our Mummy. Eve's ok, but we love you the best.'

Mum smiled and cried and laughed all at the same time.

Chapter Eight

I now pronounce you...
The Wicked Stepmother

The divorce came through six weeks later. Dad had agreed that Mum would keep the house they had lived in. Mum joked about being a free woman, but after that she spent a lot of time by herself. She didn't go out at all except to work. Her friends phoned a lot but I'd often hear her turning down invitations to meet up with them. Some weekends she didn't get out of bed until midday. I wrote in my diary.

Mum is becoming a bit of a recluse. She won't go out or see anyone. I don't know what to do. I wonder if I should tell Dad, but what can he do about it? And Mum wouldn't listen to him. She'd just start telling him it was all his fault anyway. Dad and Eve are wrapped up in planning their future. What's left for Mum? And me and Nat get to bounce between the two of them trying to be what each of them want us to be. I'm happy for Dad but sad for Mum and I can't help blaming him for making her feel this way.

The divorce itself didn't seem to make much impression on Nat, as, in many ways, things were just the same as they had been for months. We went to Dad's on Saturdays, stayed overnight and came home Sunday. Sometimes Dad came over and took us out for tea mid week. Sometimes we were one of those families sitting in MacDonald's with only their Dad. I realised that they weren't as unhappy as I'd first thought.

Some weeks later, at Dad and Eve's, they announced that they had fixed a wedding date. Actually it had been booked for a while but they hadn't plucked up the courage to tell us until now. They were getting married on Friday 19th of December. That was only two months away.

It was going to be in a Stately Home called Branstone Manor, about ten miles away in the countryside. Eve was very excited that it was going to be decorated 'all Christmasy.' She tentatively suggested that she would like Nat and I to be her bridesmaids. Despite the circumstances, that made us very excited. We wanted to know all about what we would wear and how we would do our hair. Eve showed us some designs she had been sketching for the dresses. She said her friend Siena, who would be her chief bridesmaid, had agreed to make them. Dad was pleased at our enthusiasm but did add a word of caution.

'Hang on a minute, you three. Remember we do have to get Mum's permission girls, especially since it will be the last day of term.'

'Do you think she might say no Dad?' I asked.

'I hope not, but we'll just have to play it carefully.'

When we asked her, Mum wasn't very co operative. She sighed, closed her eyes, rubbed her hands over her face and went to sit down. We all followed her. She sat there frowning and thinking.

'Well Mum, can we, please?' I finally asked.

'Oh I don't know. What about school? It's the last day of term. Won't you have parties and plays and things?'

'Not on the last day. We don't do anything useful on the last day, just tidying up. It's pretty boring.'

'And how much are these dresses going to cost me? If she's having them custom made they'll cost a fortune!'

'Eve's designed them herself and her friend Siena is making them, so you won't have to pay much Mum,' Nat explained.

'You won't have to pay for anything, Linda, 'Dad said. 'I'd never expect you to.'

'Huh, it must be costing you a fortune! Stately Home, designer dresses!'

'Look it's not too bad, okay!' Dad replied, trying not to get angry with Mum. 'We're not going on an expensive honeymoon or anything: A weekend in the Highlands. And we're not having many guests.'

'You could come and see us doing our part, Mum. You'd love our dresses,' Nat enthused.

We all stared at her and she realised her mistake. She blushed.

'Please let us do it,' I begged.

'I'll think about it,' was all Mum would say. We had to be content with that.

As Dad left he added, 'Well please don't take too long thinking about it. Eve needs to know for the dresses. Be reasonable, Linda, I'd really love the girls to do this.'

'I said I'll think about it. Now you'd better go before I start being unreasonable.'

When he had gone Nat went on at Mum even more until Mum shouted, 'Just leave it Natalie!' and stormed upstairs.

Over the next week I told Nat to keep quiet about it to Mum. She did try but now and again the odd 'Please Mum' slipped out. At school I had been keeping Zoe informed about all that was going on. She thought the dresses sounded so cool. Eve's was going to be very simple: White, sleeveless and clingy with a small train. She was going to have a tiara and a white cloak with fur trim too. (Fake of course!) Our dresses, presuming Mum relented, were going to be apple red and full length with very thin straps and silver embroidery on the bodice. Eve had said my black hair would look stunning with red. We were going to have gloves that came over our elbows, dainty shoes to match our dresses and white stoles to throw round our shoulders. We would also have diamante headbands. Eve told me she was also going to get me a diamante nose stud to match hers. She showed us the designs she and Siena had drawn. The room was going to be decorated with candles and holly. There would be white and red roses and an enormous Christmas tree in the entrance hall. We were going to sing Christmas Carols too.

'It sounds so magical,' Zoe mused. 'Can I come?'

'Hey maybe you could. I'll ask Eve. I hope it snows.'

'It would be pretty mean if your Mum didn't let you do it,' Zoe added, reminding me of the real situation.

'I know. I really hope she lets us.'

'She's jealous of Eve,' Zoe said.

'No she's not. Don't be stupid. It's just all happening so soon. It's hard for her. But I still hope she says we can do it.'

Mum gave in by the end of the week. Eve was thrilled.

'It means so much to me. Tell your Mum I really appreciate it.'

The time flew by until the big day. Dad and Eve said I could invite Zoe, and Natalie invited her best friend Sam. Our head teachers allowed us all the day off school. Zoe's form tutor, and mine, Miss. Watson, said we must bring in the photos after Christmas.

On the big day Dad came and picked us up at 9am. Our dresses were at his house. Mum was very quiet and it felt strange as Dad came to the door. They didn't speak to each other and avoided eye contact.

Mum gave us a kiss and a bigger hug than normal. 'Bye.' That was all she could manage. She closed the door and didn't even wave to us like she normally would. The excitement I had been feeling up 'til now tripped over the guilt and fell flat on its face.

Dad was determined to make sure the whole day was positive and happy. In the car, he laughed and joked and told us funny stories; like how Eve was petrified of having her dress tucked in her knickers as she walked to the front! And she had rehearsed 'I do' about a million times in the last week! He soon had us laughing and my excitement picked itself up.

Eve wasn't at the house. She had gone to stay with her Mum over night. I wondered what the point of this was when they had been living together for a long time, but I didn't ask. There were a few hours to kill before we needed to get ready as the ceremony wasn't starting until 4pm. Eve had wanted it to be getting dark outside. She'd said it would help create an atmosphere with the lighted candles. It wasn't snowing like I had hoped, but I didn't really mind.

We got into our bridesmaid dresses. Fortunately Eve's friend Siena came round to help otherwise goodness knows what we would have turned out like under Dad's management. Then a girl called Tina turned up. She said Eve had booked her to style our hair. Dad looked a bit bemused but he let her in and she did a fantastic job. Nat and I couldn't believe our eyes when we looked in the mirror and saw glamorous models staring back. Then Dad came in dressed in his morning suit. He looked great; younger too and very happy. Siena fussed over his collar and cuffs and patted his bottom a few times! (To smooth out creases she said!) Tina put some gel in his hair and spiked it up a bit. That made us laugh, but he did look quite cool when they'd finished. Finally we were ready to go. There was no posh car to take us, but Dad had polished his car and put ribbons on it to make it look all weddingy!

We got to Branstone Manor before anyone else arrived. Dad had a few things to see to. His brother, Uncle Steve, had driven up from London to be his best man and he was waiting for Dad outside the front door. We chatted for a short while, but it was cold so he took us inside and bought us a coke each while he and Dad sorted things out. The place was gorgeous. There was a huge Christmas tree in the entrance hall reaching almost to the ceiling. It was beautifully decorated and already shimmering with tiny bulbs in the fading light. There were old-fashioned lanterns all around waiting to be lit and holly and ivy strewn everywhere. It was magical. Dad was soon back to escort us to the room where the ceremony was to take place.

'Everyone okay?' he asked beaming nervously at us.

We nodded. The room was not too big, but was brilliantly decorated. There were lanterns and tea lights everywhere, mingled with all sorts of white and red flowers and lengths of trailing ivy. Several of the hotel staff were in the process of lighting all the candles. Quite a few people were milling around now. We saw Dad's other brother, Mark with Auntie Julie and our cousins. There were a few of Dad's friends that I recognised. Then we saw Granddad.

'Well aren't you the belles of the ball,' he chuckled, kissing us.

Next Zoe arrived. She spotted us and she came straight over.

'You look ace!' she cried. 'The dresses look even better in real life than I'd imagined! And this place is so cool!'

I giggled. 'Maybe I am in Cinderella after all!'

She giggled. I showed her where to sit.

Soon most of the seats were full. The celebrant was ready at the front. She had a chat with Nat and I, making us feel more relaxed. Dad and Uncle Steve were fidgeting nervously on the chairs at the front of the room. A dreamy melody was floating from a harp played by another of Eve's friends. People were chatting quietly. Nat and I went to wait at the back. Then Siena hurried in from the entrance hall whispering to us that Eve had arrived. We were ushered outside to meet her. She looked beautiful. Her long black hair had been set in soft curls falling gently round her face. Her dress hugged her slim figure perfectly. The cloak and tiara made her look like the Snow Queen. She grinned and headed straight for us, arms outstretched.

'Mind the dresses!' I said.

'You look gorgeous!' she exclaimed.

'So do you,' we both said at once and we all giggled.

'Photographs please,' interrupted the photographer. We stood inside by the tree. After several shots it was time.

'Are you ready?' smiled Eve. We nodded nervously.

Siena popped her head round the door to let them know and gave us the thumbs up. Eve squeezed our hands and we made our entrance.

The room had been darkened so that the lights of the candles and lanterns flickered romantically. The harpist played as we walked slowly to the front of the room, smiling at everyone. Dad's mouth hung open and when we reached the front I could see tears in his eyes. Eve and Dad held hands and beamed at each other. Then the celebrant began the ceremony. We sang Eve's favourite carol, 'In the Bleak Mid Winter' at the beginning, and Dad's favourite carol, 'O Come All Ye Faithful' at the end. Before we knew it the celebrant was saying, 'I now pronounce you man and wife. You may kiss the bride.' But Dad was already kissing the bride!

Afterwards there were lots more photos and then the meal. It was like a big Christmas dinner, with party poppers and party hats and everyone telling the jokes from the crackers. The speeches made the adults laugh a lot and go all gooey.

'When does the disco start?' Nat whispered to me while Eve was making a speech.

'Not for ages,' I whispered back. I glanced over at Zoe who was yawning behind her napkin.

The disco was the best bit. Zoe and I danced to nearly every song. 'Well you've really done it now!' she shouted in my ear as we danced.

'Done what?' I shouted back.

'Gone and got yourself a Wicked Stepmother!'

I gave her a playful shove. She shoved me back. I fell over. She tripped over me and we ended up in a laughing heap on the dance floor.

By the end of the evening we were exhausted. At eleven o'clock Dad told us we needed to get ready to go home. Uncle Steve was going to take us. Dad and Eve were staying at the Manor for the night. Nat and I went up to a bedroom where we could get changed. As we took off our bridesmaid dresses it was like stripping the magic away. Suddenly I felt normal again as we stood there in our jeans looking in the full length mirror.

'I don't want to go home,' said Nat's reflection.

'Me neither,' mine agreed.

'Don't go on about it to Mum,' I said.

'I won't.'

'It's weird, isn't it?'

'Yeah.'

Uncle Steve knocked on the door. 'Ready?'

'Coming,' I shouted.

We went to kiss Dad and Eve goodbye. Eve had changed out of her wedding dress earlier in the evening. She was wearing a long black evening dress which made her look very elegant – and older I thought.

'I've got something for you.' She handed us each a small box, elegantly wrapped in silver paper with a ribbon tied around it. 'You can open them now,' she said seeing our hesitation. Inside each was a silver locket with intricate Celtic knot work on the front. My name was inscribed on the back of mine and Nat's on hers.

'They're beautiful. Thank you,' I said.

'Thank you,' Nat echoed. Eve beamed.

'Hope all goes well at home,' Dad offered. 'Bye sweet hearts.' They kissed us and waved us off as we left in Uncle Steve's car.

When Mum opened the door she was smiling. Well, her mouth was smiling. She talked briefly with Uncle Steve, then we said goodbye to him and went inside.

'How did it go then?' she asked.

Nat and I looked hesitantly at each other. 'Fine,' I said.

'Did you have a good time?'

'Yes,' Nat replied.

'I bet you two were beautiful.'

'We looked like princesses Mum.' Nat offered, a bit too enthusiastically. I gave her a look.

'Well, that's good then,' sighed Mum. 'Time for bed I think. You must be tired.'

It was midnight.

Chapter Nine

Out of the Blue

The next morning we woke up late. I stayed in bed to write my diary.

Yesterday Dad and Eve got married. It was a great day. Me and Nat looked ace in our bridesmaids' dresses. Can't wait to see the photos. Eve and Dad looked fab too. Was a bit nervous for the ceremony, but didn't do anything embarrassing.

The disco was wicked. Me and Zoe were so tired after dancing for about three hours. No one danced as much as we did. Dad grinned all day. He kept hugging me and Nat and asking us if we were having a good time.

I was a bit sad when we had to go back to mum's though. Felt like Dad was leaving us behind. I know that was just stupid now though. This morning he and Eve are off to Scotland on their honeymoon until Boxing Day.

Dad sent us a postcard. Somehow it managed to get to us despite the Christmas post. Nat picked it up and came running to show me. She read it out.

'Dear Nat and Lou,

Having a lovely, chilly time here in Scotland. The mountains are beautiful in the snow. Been skiing today. Didn't break a leg. Phew! Can't wait to see you on 27th. All my love, Dad.'

No mention of Eve. 'Can I see it please?' I took the card from Nat and read it myself. I turned it over to look at the white peaks against a brilliant blue sky. I read it again.

'Can I put it in my room Lou?' asked Nat.

'Yeah, go on then,' I smiled.

We were busy getting ready for Christmas. There was last minute shopping to do, Christmas cooking with Mum and a couple of parties to fit in. Christmas Day was on the Thursday. Mum made sure lots of relatives came round to share Christmas dinner with us, but we there was an empty space even though all the chairs were filled. So much had happened since that day, nearly a year ago, when Dad had blurted out, 'I'm leaving.'

Uncle Eddie organised the silly party games as usual after lunch. He thinks it's hilarious to pass a bin liner round the circle filled with old clothes. When the music stops you have to take an item out and put it on until the bag is empty. Then everyone has to do the conga round the house looking ridiculous. The adults laugh so much they have to sit down for half an hour, exhausted, when the game is finished. We also had to play pass the parcel, charades and Who's Who. As soon as we could, the kids sneaked off upstairs to watch one of our new DVDs. The adults carried on playing.

I wrote in my diary that night and saw what I'd written only a few days ago about the wedding. I wished Dad was here.

On 27th we went to Dad and Eve's in the afternoon. It was like Christmas Day all over again, with a whole new set of presents (lots of Scottish ones!). Dad was so pleased to see us. He threw his arms around us and held us tight for far too long. There were just the four of us but we had a good time. We had a buffet tea. No leftover turkey thankfully, as Dad and Eve had gone out for Christmas dinner. We played a new board game after tea that Dad had bought us. Then Eve lit lots of candles and we crashed out and watched good old Mary Poppins again. Nat fell asleep. Both of us were cuddled in to Dad. Too soon we had to leave. It had been a cosy, lazy day. Strangely, it had felt like we were a family, the four of us.

The rest of the holiday was spent with Mum. I saw Zoe a few times and we went into town to look in the sales and spend some Christmas money. Nat and I didn't see Dad and Eve because Dad had said we should really be with Mum.

On the Monday before school started back Mum was sitting at the breakfast table with a letter in her hand. She had a very serious look on her face as she stared hard at the letter.

'What's up, Mum?' I asked coming into the kitchen.

She looked up as if I'd startled her. 'What? Oh, hi love. Er, nothing's up. Would you like some toast?' She slid the letter half under the other post and got up.

'Yes please,' I answered, looking at the corner of the letter peeping out. 'Are you sure there's nothing up? It's just that you looked really worried when you were looking at that letter.'

'Oh, did I? Just concentrating. Something I didn't quite understand.'

Later I caught her again staring at the letter.

'Mum,' I said, 'Please tell me what's wrong.'

'There's nothing wrong, love. It's fine.' She held the letter behind her back. Did she think I was seven years old?

'Yes there is. It's that letter. I'm not stupid Mum. It's something bad isn't it?'

She looked at me for a while, biting her lip. Then she looked at the letter. 'Oh well, you'll find out sooner or later. I just didn't know how you'd take it. And you seemed to be getting on so well with her. I can't understand it.'

'What? Who?'

'You'd better read it for yourself, then you'll really believe it. I can't take it in, but maybe you can make sense of it.' She handed me the type written letter. I read it.

Dear Linda,

I want you to know something, which must be kept between ourselves. It will be for your benefit as well as mine, I'm sure you'll agree. Up until now I have been very nice to your daughters. In fact we have been getting along very well indeed, at least as far as they're aware. They really like me and we've bonded so well you wouldn't believe it. However, I never wanted your children and now I've got Mike I'd like them out of my life as far as possible. So you must make excuses to Mike as to why they can't come here. He can obviously come to you and take them out but I don't want to be bothered with them anymore. I realise in the long term we will need to rethink the strategy but for now this will have to do. If you don't want to help me in this remember your girls really like me and I could get them to like me a LOT more, believe me! I'm sure you don't want to lose out to their stepmother, do you? If you tell Mike any of this I will make your life a misery.

I hope you will see the benefits of co-operating.

Eve

I couldn't believe it. I had to read it several times to take it in. Even then I was speechless. Mum looked anxiously at me.

'I don't know what to say. She had me fooled too, love. I thought she genuinely liked you and Natalie. I don't know what to do.'

'We've got to tell Dad,' I said immediately. 'He'll have it out with her. She was just stringing us along. How could she be so convincing? That's evil! The witch! The lying, scheming, two faced, evil witch!' I could feel tears stinging my eyes now. Mum came and hugged me.

'Do you think we should tell Nat?' she asked, as if I would know what to do.

'I don't .....'

'Tell me what?' said Nat coming into the room. 'What's the matter? Why is Lou crying?'

Mum and I looked at each other, not knowing what to do. I decided. 'It's Eve. She's been lying to us all along. She doesn't really like us. She hates us in fact. She doesn't want us to go to Dad's anymore.'

'Not go to Dad's?' Nat burst into tears. 'But I want to see Dad!' she wailed. 'I want to see Dad!'

It took a while for Mum to calm us down. Nat was so upset and I was so angry. Mum told us she had to play it carefully. I insisted we should tell him but she said not yet. She would handle it for a while and did we think we could play along. We nodded, a little confused. Mum seemed to be hatching her own plan.

When Dad phoned to arrange to pick us up on Saturday I heard Mum begin her story.

'Well you see Mike, Nat has been feeling really unsure about things since the wedding and Christmas, I think it would do her good if you could visit them here, or take them somewhere neutral for a while... No, I don't think they should... No, I think it should just be you. I'm sure she'll get over it. She just needs some security for a while…Thanks…Yeah! I appreciate you being so understanding.' She put the phone down and smiled to herself.

'Was that Dad, Mum?' I asked.

She hadn't noticed me standing across the hall and looked a little startled. 'Yes love, everything's sorted; for a few weeks at least. You must make sure you and Nat don't say anything about Eve. I know it'll be hard for you Lou. I know how angry you are and how much she's hurt you. I'm sure your chance to say what you think of her will come.'

I nodded.

That night I said what I thought of Eve to my diary. It took two whole pages and there were some words in there I'd never used before in my life! I didn't know if I'd actually be able to say it to her face though. I took the necklace she had given me and yanked the chain with such force that as it snapped the locket flew across the room.

'I don't want your bribery. I don't want anything you've ever given me.'

I took the photographs of the mural we'd painted together and ripped them up.

'Sucking up to us to get our dad. Witch!' I shouted across the bedroom.

Nat kept asking me why Eve didn't like us anymore. She kept thinking she'd done something wrong.

'Do you think I wasn't a very good bridesmaid?' she asked the next day, looking fondly at her locket in it's box.

'Of course you were, Nat. You were perfect. It's all to do with grown up things, complicated stuff.'

Nat walked away shaking her head and mumbling to herself. What I didn't understand was why we couldn't tell Dad. But I just had to trust Mum on this one. She seemed to have a plan herself.

At school I had been relating all this to Zoe. At first she thought it was the juiciest bit of gossip ever.

'It's like a Coronation Street plot isn't it?' she enthused. 'She really has turned out to be the Wicked Stepmother after all hasn't she? Good job your Mum is around or who knows what she would have done with you!'

'It's not funny!' I snapped. 'This is my life we're talking about not some stupid soap or, even stupider still, some fairy tale. Anyway, they have happy endings. I can't see how this will.'

'Sorry, Lou.'

'We're seeing Dad tomorrow. I don't know what we'll say to him. He thinks Eve's wonderful. Little does he know!'

'Maybe you should tell him, even if your Mum doesn't want you to.'

'No, I've promised I won't and so has Nat. We'll see what Mum's planning first.'

'Okay, but if I was you, I'd have to go round there and tell her what I thought of her.'

'Well, maybe I will in time.'

On Saturday Dad came to pick us up. He took us to this interactive arts and crafts exhibition. It was okay. There was loads to do. I made jewellery and did some batik. Nat also made jewellery and did some glass painting. I noticed Dad being particularly lovely to Nat, probably because of Mum's excuse on the phone. But in between the crafty bits, he kept talking about Eve. How she wished she could have come and she hoped we were okay. Nat and I kept giving each other knowing looks, wanting desperately to blurt it all out about the letter and how Eve was a two faced schemer. But somehow we managed to make it to the end of the day without saying anything. The atmosphere was strained and Dad felt it.

As we drove home in the car he said, 'I'm sorry it's been such an odd day. But it won't be long before you feel okay about coming to the house again will it? We do love you so much, Eve and I. But you just take all the time you need love.' He turned his head to Nat while he should have been looking at the road.

Nat smiled weakly at him and turned in panic to me. But I couldn't help because I knew if I opened my mouth it would all come out.

This went on for two more weeks. Dad would come and take us out on his own. Each time it got harder and harder as he was more and more desperate for things to get back to how they were before the wedding. He kept asking Mum if she thought Nat would be ready to come back yet or even if I could come on my own. But Mum kept putting him off with more excuses. I didn't want to see Eve ever again. I felt so hurt by her deception. And I felt a fool for being taken in by it. I didn't know how this was going to turn out. I tried to talk to Mum about it.

'We've got to tell him the truth Mum. This can't go on forever. He shouldn't be with Eve when she's such a liar. I mean what does she really want from Dad? Maybe she's plotting to bump him off and get all his money.'

'Lou, don't be so ridiculous. Anyway your Dad hasn't got any money. He must be pretty broke after the divorce settlement.'

'Well, we should still tell him about her. Show him the letter.'

'No Lou. It's tricky; a delicate situation. He won't believe me and then who knows what he'll do.' Mum would not discuss it any further and I was getting more and more frustrated with her.

'It's horrible,' I told Zoe one morning at school. 'I feel like Dad is being lied to by everyone! He hasn't a clue what's really going on. Mum seems to be taking it okay. I actually think she's quite glad we're not seeing Eve. She never liked the idea of us getting so friendly with her. She keeps fretting about how Dad will take it if he finds out the truth.'

'Well I've told you what I would do Lou. You should just have it out with him.'

'Yeah, I know.'

I thought about what Zoe kept telling me for the rest of the morning. I couldn't keep up the deception. Anyway, it couldn't go on forever. I decided to confront Mum about it that evening and tell her that I was going to tell Dad if she didn't. In the afternoon I was musing about it during geography, when the deputy head came into the classroom and asked to speak to me. I followed her down to her room. She made me sit down.

'Now Louise, I don't want you to get too worried about what I'm about to tell you because it's going to be fine.'

Panic!

'Your Mum's been in a car accident but...'

'A car accident!' I yelled, jumping to my feet.

Mrs. Evans gently put her hands on my shoulders and made me sit down again. She sat beside me.

'Yes. But she's going to be okay. She has some injuries to her leg and ribs but nothing life threatening, so she will be all right.'

My mind was racing. I could feel tears running down my cheeks. Mrs. Evans gave me some tissues and put her arm round my shoulders.

'Your Dad has been informed and has gone to fetch your sister. Then he's coming to get you and take you to the hospital. I shouldn't think he'll be long so you just wait here. I'm going to get you a glass of water.'

She left the room. The tears kept coming and in my head I just kept shouting out for Mum. Mrs. Evans came back with the water. I sipped it and wiped my eyes. She talked to me the whole time reassuring me that my Mum was going to be okay. Dad arrived after about ten minutes, but it felt more like ten hours.

'Lou. Are you all right? Come on love, let's get to the hospital, then you'll be able to see your Mum. She's going to be okay.' He bundled me out of the door saying thanks to Mrs. Evans as he went.

Nat was in the car. She had been crying. She clung to me as I got in. I found myself now to be the one saying 'It's going to be all right.' Dad was trying to be reassuring as he drove but I could tell he was anxious.

'I have spoken to them at the hospital and she is going straight to theatre for an operation on her leg. So we won't be able to see her straight away, but the doctors will be able to tell us what's going on.'

When we arrived at the hospital we were ushered into a 'relative's room.' A very nice doctor explained that Mum had no critical injuries and that she would be 100% back to normal when she recovered. She had broken her leg and cracked some ribs and had a few cuts and bruises. Apparently she had pulled out of a parking space at the side of the road without looking and a car had gone into her. The car was a write-off but thankfully Mum wasn't.

We sat around for what seemed like an endless time in the waiting area in the corridor. We drank lots of vending machine drinks and ate junk food. Finally we were allowed to see Mum. By this time it was mid evening. Mum was sleeping on the ward. She looked a bit bruised but much better than I'd expected her to.

We were allowed to give her a gentle kiss.

'We'll come back tomorrow,' whispered Dad, 'so you can speak to her. We'd better go back to your place and get some things, and then we'll go back to mine. I phoned Eve before I picked you up. She said she'd get your beds ready. She'll be relieved to hear everything's going to be okay.'

It hadn't dawned on us until now that we would have to stay at Dad's while Mum was in hospital.

'But, we can't stay at yours!' I blurted out. 'Not after... Mum wouldn't.... Eve....'

Dad looked confused and who could blame him when he had no idea what I was trying not to tell him!

'It'll be okay. I know things have been difficult lately, especially for you Nat, but maybe it will help you to feel at home with us again, if you have to stay with us for a while. You'll remember all the things you liked about staying over at our house.'

'I don't want to. Please Dad. You come and stay at home till Mum gets back, please,' Nat begged.

'It will be okay love, I promise,' he said scooping her up and giving her a kiss. 'Come on, it's been a traumatic day for you both. Let's go and leave Mum in peace 'til tomorrow.'

We went back home and picked up some things for the next few days. I had a key so we were able to get in. While we were in our bedrooms I whispered to Nat to just go straight to bed when we got there. We just wouldn't speak to Eve.

When we arrived at Dad's house Eve greeted us with arms open ready to hug us. She was full of comforting, sympathetic words that meant nothing. I turned away as she tried to hug me and Nat hid behind me. Eve said we must be shattered and what a terrible ordeal we'd had, then she went to make us a drink. I told Dad that we just wanted to go to bed. So we went upstairs and he brought us up a hot chocolate before we fell into an exhausted sleep.

Chapter Ten

The truth will out

The next day I woke early, anxious to see Mum. It was 6:30 and no one else was awake. I had brought my diary with me and wanted to record the events of the previous day. I crept downstairs so I could put a light on to write.

A terrible thing has happened. Mum had a car crash yesterday and she's in hospital. She is going to be okay thankfully. I'd been planning to have an argument with her about Dad and the letter when I got home last night. Imagine if she had died yesterday! I really want to speak to her today. And now we're staying at Eve's and she is pretending to be all kind and sympathetic, but I saw the frown she gave Dad when she thought we weren't looking. She definitely doesn't want us here.

I had almost finished when, from behind me, Eve's voice said, 'Hi Lou. How are you this morning?'

I didn't even look up. I slammed my diary shut. 'Fine!' I walked past her upstairs back to my room. I lay on the bottom bunk in the dark for a while. I could hear Nat breathing heavily above me. Maybe this would be the time to tell Eve what I thought of her. Get it out in the open. But then we'd have to live here for who knew how many days having blurted all that out. I couldn't do it. I felt paralysed. Then Zoe's voice started seeping through the darkness. *'You should tell her what you think of her!'*

'I can't!' said my voice in my head.

'You should tell her!' insisted Zoe.

'I can't! I hissed.

'Tell her!' Zoe shouted.

I got out of bed and walked determinedly to the kitchen where I could hear Eve moving around. The radio was on and she was singing. My stomach was churning. She had her back to me as I came to the door.

'I really don't get you,' I said, standing in the doorway with my arms folded.

She turned round. 'Sorry?' she smiled. Then she looked shocked as she saw my face.

'You should be!' I said. 'You should be sorry, but you're not. You're acting like you've done nothing wrong! But you don't fool me. I know the truth.' I was trying hard to handle it like I thought Zoe would.

'Have I? If I have done something wrong I need to know what it is so I can put it right.' she said, coming towards me, looking pale. 'Come and sit down Louise and we can talk.'

How could she act so innocently? I refused to sit down but she did.

'You wrote my Mum that scheming letter and you say you don't know what you've done!' I was beginning to raise my voice.

'What letter?'

'You know very well what letter. Why don't you stop pretending!'

'Lou, I don't know what you're talking about. What was in the letter.'

'You know what! How you never liked me and Nat. You just used us to get Dad. Now you don't want to see us and you don't want Dad to know what a two faced cow you are!' I shouted the last bit at her, though I couldn't quite bring myself to call her what Zoe had suggested.

At this point Dad came down the stairs. 'What's going on?' he asked through bleary eyes.

Now I was scared and it suddenly dawned on me what I'd done. But I was in too deep to stop. 'Ask her about the letter she wrote Mum.'

'What letter?' Dad said.

'I don't know what she means,' said Eve. 'She says I wrote a nasty letter to Linda saying I didn't want to see the girls; that I'd just been using them to get you or something like that.'

Dad looked from Eve to me, confused. He rubbed his hands over his face and through his hair. He pushed past me and went to sit down at the kitchen table.

'What's this all about Lou? Is this something to do with why you haven't been coming round over the last few weeks?'

'Yes. Mum said we should keep quiet about it and she would sort it out. Eve told her to keep quiet. She was blackmailing Mum!'

'Mike, you must believe I'd never do such a thing. It's ridiculous. I've really missed the girls!'

Nat came down at this point. She just stood listening to what was going on.

'I do believe you sweetheart,' Dad said to Eve. 'But there must be some explanation, Lou wouldn't make this up.'

'The explanation is she fooled us all Dad. She's been stringing us along from the start.'

'Lou, I did not write a letter to your Mum and I genuinely do care for you and Nat. I am telling the truth.' Her eyes pleaded with mine. For a fleeting moment I wanted to believe her.

As if reading my mind she said, 'You've got to believe me. I know you're not making it up about the letter, but there's no way on earth I would do such a horrible thing! Someone else must have written it. Someone who's got it in for me, but I've no idea who.'

'I think she's telling the truth,' Nat suddenly piped up. We all looked at her. She was standing in the hallway, with her hands on her hips looking very serious.

'I am, Nat, I am. Thank you for believing me. Lou

please, listen. I am telling the truth.'

'Why do you believe her Nat? She's just pretending again because Dad is here.'

'I don't think she is. She's always been nice to us. It doesn't make sense.'

There was a long, long pause. They all stared at me.

'Well if you didn't write it then...... we need to find out who did,' I said.

Eve's eyes began to fill up. 'I won't rest until it's proved to you that I didn't do this. I couldn't hurt you or your Dad like that.' Dad squeezed her hand. Then he came over to Nat and I.

'We will get to the bottom of this,' he reassured us. 'But now we should get dressed and go and see Mum.'

As I turned to go upstairs I glanced back at Eve. She was sitting with her head in her hands staring at the table. I was still suspicious.

On the way to the hospital no one said much. When we got there we put on our cheeriest faces. Mum was sitting up in bed and when she saw us she beamed. We ran up to the bed and almost fell on top of her trying to hug her.

'Careful,' Dad laughed. Then we all started speaking at once, trying to tell her how relieved we were that she was okay. She just smiled and laughed and said, 'Oooh, that hurts.' And 'Don't make me laugh!' She told us a bit about the accident and how she felt really stupid, but grateful to be alive. Her first words when she came round after the operation were about us and where we were staying. She said she hoped it wasn't too much trouble for Dad. She was sorry to have caused such worry. She babbled on for ages, but we all just said, 'Aw don't be silly Mum!' and 'Its okay Mum,' and 'don't worry about a thing Linda.' It was a huge relief all round to see her so perky, if a little battered and bruised. Nat asked when she'd be coming home.

'Well they told me this morning that I'd have to stay in for at least a week to rest,' Mum frowned. 'So I guess you'll have to stay with Dad, I'm sorry to put you out, Mike.' She bit her lip.

'It's no trouble at all,' Dad reassured her. 'It's a treat for Eve and I to have the girls. You just get lots of rest and we'll do all we can to make sure you get better quickly. Won't we girls?'

We nodded enthusiastically. Mum looked a bit anxious.

'So with that in mind, we should leave your Mum to rest. We'll come back tomorrow with a few bunches of grapes and a couple of bottles of Lucozade!'

We all laughed and kissed Mum goodbye.

Over the next few days we went to visit Mum every evening. Her cheeks grew rosier and she seemed a little less tired each day. Dad had insisted that we shouldn't miss too much school. Everyone wanted to hear all the details of what had happened to Mum. I was the most popular girl to talk to until the novelty wore off.

Zoe was intrigued by the letter mystery. She wanted to play detective and solve it of course.

'Do you really think Eve didn't write it then?'

'I'm fairly convinced. Being with her again has made me realise I like her. It's hard to believe it's all an act, she's too....genuine,' I mused. 'We've gone round and round in circles trying to work out who could have written it.'

'Well, who has it in for her? Or maybe they've got it in for your Mum.'

'But how would this hurt Mum? It doesn't make her look bad, only Eve.'

'Yes but it has made your Mum lie to your Dad. And maybe they knew that sooner or later it would all have to come out. No, maybe it's your Dad they want to get!'

She was totally absorbed in it now. 'Whoa! Slow down Miss. Marple! It's too confusing!' Just then the buzzer sounded for next lesson so we went our separate ways. I could think of nothing else throughout the whole of the afternoon.

Back at Dad's, things were still a little awkward. There was an atmosphere of tension between us and Eve. That night Eve announced that she would like to go and see Mum. We all looked at her in shock.

'Oh I'm not sure that would be a good idea, sweetheart,' said Dad.

'I really need to talk to her about this letter,' Eve insisted. 'I don't want her to think badly of me. I'd like her to know I'm actually concerned about her too. And most of all we could kick around some ideas about who might have written the letter.'

'I don't think it would go down well at the moment.'

'What do you think girls?' asked Eve.

At first we shook our heads. Dad still wasn't sure that this was the best circumstances for Eve and Mum to meet for the first time.

Eve thought for a moment then said, 'Well neither am I, but I need to do this sooner rather than later, so I'm going to go tomorrow.'

We nodded apprehensively.

The next day my stomach whirled like a tumble dryer. I knew what time Eve was going to see Mum. It was during science, just after double maths. I hate maths at the best of times but this morning I had to leave the room because I thought I was going to be sick. As I stood in the toilets I had a thought. Maybe if I caught a bus straight away I could go down to the hospital and try to smooth things between Mum and Eve. I'd never bunked off school in my life so I felt even sicker. I went back to my lesson and asked the teacher if I could go to the medical room. As I really did look white and about to throw up he didn't have any objection. I headed furtively out of the side door and within five minutes I was on a bus to the hospital. It was so easy. The bus seemed to take ages. Loads of people wanted to get on and off at every stop. I felt like a fugitive. I zipped my coat up to try and hide my school uniform. I was taking deep breaths to try and combat the nausea that kept rising from my stomach. A woman asked me if I was ok.

'I'm just feeling a bit sick,' I said.

'Here you are love, have a mint. I always suck one if I'm feeling a bit travel sick. It's these buses they lurch about all over the place.'

I took the mint and thanked her. It did help. I was glad to emerge from the bus and gulp some fresh air though. It was only a few minutes walk to the hospital but I realised Eve would have been there for some time now. What if she'd chickened out? I'd have to go in and find out. I'd only just got inside the main entrance when I saw Eve hurrying towards me. She had her head down and didn't see me at first.

'Eve!' I called.

She looked up. Her face was pale but as she recognised me it flushed.

'Louise! What are you doing here? Why aren't you at school?'

'I couldn't bear it. I had to come and see what was going on between you and Mum. I thought I might be able to help. Have you seen her?'

'Yes. Yes we've talked. Look we should phone your Dad and get him to take you back to school. You'll get into real trouble if we don't go sort it out.'

'No. I want to know what happened with you and Mum. Did you get to the bottom of it? Is she upset? Should I go and see her?'

Eve looked flustered. 'I don't think you should go in to her now. She needs some time on her own.'

'Why? What have you said to her? Have you upset her? You better not have. Dad was right you shouldn't have come.'

She went to put her arm round me. I shrugged away. 'Come on. I'm going to call your Dad.'

'No please don't. He'll kill me. I'll go back to school. They think I'm in the medical room. No one will suspect anything: Its organised chaos there. You still haven't told me about the letter.'

'I can't Lou.' She hesitated, fiddling with her handbag. 'You need to talk about it together, with your Mum and Dad here. You're coming back here this evening with him aren't you?'

'Yes, but why can't you tell me? Something awful's happened. I know it. Just tell me!'

Eve was nearly in tears. 'You shouldn't have come, Louise. I'm taking you back to school. I won't tell your Dad you were here, but you've got to wait 'til later for explanations.'

We got on the bus together and sat in silence all the way back to school. It was lunchtime when we got there.

'Are you sure you will be ok? I'll come and make excuses for you if you like?'

'I'll be fine!' I snapped and stormed back into school.

When Dad picked me up from school I looked at

Nat in the back of the car. She was white as a sheet and I felt terrified. Dad made reassuring noises all the way to the hospital, but at the same time he kept rubbing his eyebrows and I could see him biting his lip through the mirror.

Chapter Eleven

Revelations

As we walked onto the ward we put on our best plastic smiles but trembled inside. Mum was staring straight ahead. She wasn't looking for us eagerly like she normally did at this time in the evening. We came round the bottom of her bed putting on the chirpiest voices we could muster to say hi. I was about to kiss her, but she looked at us like a frightened rabbit. Then she looked down at the bed clothes and began to sob. Dad quickly drew the curtains round the bed.

'What's wrong Mum? What is it? Did Eve upset you?' I blurted out. Nat flung her arms round Mum's neck and Dad sat down next to the bed. Mum continued to sob. She put her hand over her mouth to try and stifle the noise. It was very loud. A nurse popped her head round and asked if Mum needed her. Mum shook her head and Dad said we just needed some time alone. Dad gave Mum the tissue box. She blew her nose several times and dabbed her eyes.

'I'm so sorry,' she sobbed. 'You will all hate me.'

We looked puzzled. Then Nat said, 'Don't be silly Mum, we love you.' She clung tightly to Mum's neck and kissed her cheek several times.

'Yes, you will. You'll hate me,' she sniffed.

'I'm sorry Linda. I should have stopped Eve from coming. She's really upset you and you don't need all this while you're trying to recover.'

'It's not her fault,' Mum sniveled. 'She hasn't done anything wrong. I'm sorry. I've been so mean about her. I never gave her a chance.'

The three of us looked at each other in wonder. Dad tried to be soothing. 'Oh it's understandable. It's been a really hard year for you. You mustn't feel bad, it's my fault if anyone's. It's certainly not yours.'

She looked into each of our faces with frightened eyes. Then she focused on the curtain straight ahead. 'I wrote the letter. At least, I got a friend to type it and post it, but I told her exactly what to write.' There was a pause as we all looked at Mum in shock. 'I wanted to make Eve look really bad. I hated her getting so close to the girls. I hated her for breaking up my family. I hated her for having a fairytale wedding. I didn't really know how I was going to keep up the pretence. It was stupid and malicious.'

She started crying again. No one could speak. She struggled to regain some composure. 'When Eve came to see me today I was pretty rude to her. I told her to get out and I was about to call a nurse and have her removed. And then she started talking about the letter. I wanted to slink under the bed clothes and hide. I tried to get her to go away but she wouldn't and as she talked I began to realise how much she cared about you all; even me for some strange reason. She wanted to find out who could have done such a thing at such a fragile time. The more she spoke, the worse I felt until I just broke down and told her the whole story. I thought she'd storm off and I'd find myself fighting a custody battle soon, but she didn't. She kept reassuring me that she didn't want to take my place and never could. We talked for a long time about things. I felt so foolish. But you know what? For the first time since we split up I felt ....relieved.'

I heard words, slow and menacing coming out of my mouth. 'How could you do it, Mum? You made us think such despicable things about Eve and it was you all the time!' My voice rose in pitch as anger overcame me. 'I thought Dad was the rotten one for leaving you and us to be with Eve. I never could understand how he could do it. But this! You are just as bad! You lied to us; you kept us from seeing as much of Dad as we could have.'

I got up, angrily wiping tears from my eyes and marched out of the ward. I could hear Nat saying, 'It'll be ok Mum. You didn't mean it. Don't cry Mum.'

The last thing I heard was Mum. 'Go after her Mike, please. Poor Lou. She's right.'

Dad caught up with me in the corridor. He grabbed my arm. 'Lou. Stop.'

'I'm not going back in Dad. I can't face her right now. I don't know what to say.'

'It's ok, love. It's fine to be angry. I bet you felt the same about me a year ago.'

'I did.'

'Well you gave me a chance. You were wonderful. You've taken it so well. Now you've got to give your mum a chance. I know we're asking a lot of you and Nat. but please try. Mum needs you.'

'She needed you Dad but it didn't stop you doing what you wanted.'

He winced. 'That's true. I've no right to be asking you to do something I wasn't prepared to do. I don't know what else to say.'

We sat down on the blue plastic chairs in the corridor. There was silence for a long time. The past year or so was playing out on the wall in front of me like a film. I looked at Dad. His brow was furrowed but there was always gentleness in his eyes.

'I'd better go back in.' He hesitated but I continued to stare ahead.

I thought I'd never really understand what had gone on between him and Mum, or the reasons why he had chosen to leave. I thought about Mum. I tried to understand why she had deceived us in such a way. If I'd forgiven Dad then maybe I had to do the same for Mum. I didn't go back into the ward that day.

When we got back to Dad's I waited until Eve was alone in the kitchen. She was washing the dishes. I walked over to the sink and took up a tea towel. We worked in awkward silence for a few minutes, while I tried to form an adequate sentence.

'Eve?'

'Yes.'

'I'm sorry.'

'Accepted,' she said.

Then she turned to me and grinned. I had a sudden urge to hug her. So I did.

In a few days time Mum was going to be able to come home. She would have to take it easy and we were going to have to be really helpful, but that was fine. A rota of jobs was drawn up. We were also going to spend a bit more time at Dad and Eve's to give Mum some peace. Eve had been to see Mum a couple of times since her first visit. She and Mum seemed to be finding it helpful.

'Shall we throw a welcome home party do you think?' Eve suggested hesitantly, that evening while we were eating supper.

'Yeah!' Nat cheered, her eyes lighting up.

I smiled.

Dad agreed that it would make Mum feel very loved which was what she needed at the moment. So we started planning it. We'd have a banner on a really long piece of material, which Eve, Nat and I would paint. Eve would make some of her gorgeous cakes and Nat and I might help! We'd go shopping tomorrow night for some other food, and then there were the guests. It was a bit short notice, but the more people we could get the better. So Dad took us home to get Mum's phone book and we phoned as many of Mum's friends as we could. I also phoned Zoe and a few of my friends and so did Nat. By the end of the evening twenty people had said they could come.

When the day came, Mum was allowed to leave the hospital after 3 o'clock in the afternoon, when she had been discharged. Most people couldn't make it for the party until 5:30 so Dad made up some excuse as to why he couldn't pick Mum up until five. Eve had gone round to the house the previous day and got almost everything set up and ready. Today she just had to do one or two things like putting the banner up. Dad, Nat and I went to pick Mum up.

'What a relief to get out of this place!' gasped Mum as we left. 'Don't get me wrong, the staff are wonderful but as Dorothy would say, 'there's no place like home!'

We laughed and bundled Mum –gently – into the car. She needed lots of room as her leg was in plaster and she had crutches to lean on as she hopped along. Dad put those in the boot though. As we pulled into the street we could see the banner clearly declaring to the world, in rainbow colours, 'We love you Mum!' She gasped and put her hands to her face.

When the car stopped people poured out of the house to greet her. We felt like royalty. Dad helped Mum to her feet and supported her as she tried to walk. Mum looked up at the banner and all around her at the crowd of smiling faces shouting messages of welcome. I could see she was overwhelmed.

'Oh, thank you everyone. This is so amazing. That banner, it's beautiful. What a lovely surprise, thank you.' She hugged Nat. Then she turned to me. Today was the first time I'd seen her since her confession. She put her arms out to me. After a momentary hesitation I let her hug me.

'Eve helped us make the banner. In fact the whole thing was her idea,' explained Nat.

'No, not really. The girls did most of it,' Eve said, blushing.

'Well it's wonderful,' smiled Mum turning back to Eve. 'Thank you.'

'Come on let's go inside and eat and dance!' announced Eve. 'Ah, or maybe just eat,' she smiled looking at Mum.

The food was great. There was loads of it. Everyone was making yummy noises over Eve's cakes. Most people were mingling and chatting and fussing over Mum. Not many were dancing I have to say, just Nat and her friends. Even they were mainly giggling and falling on the floor. If I didn't know better I would have thought they'd been drinking.

Dad was chatting to Mum. They were sitting on the sofa watching Nat's antics and smiling as they talked. They looked like old friends. I couldn't figure them out really. Eve was in the kitchen talking to lots of different people as she made sure everyone was okay for drinks. It was weird. Zoe had been talking to her about the wedding and the letter and all the stuff I didn't want her to bring up right now.

'She's pretty cool your Wicked Stepmother,' she said coming over to me.

'What makes you say that?' I laughed, thinking of all the horrible things Zoe had spouted about Eve over the past months.

'Well, after what your Mum did. I know she had her reasons; you can't blame her. And I do like your Mum. But Eve's been so great about it. In fact I'd say she's been wicked.'

We both looked at each other and burst out laughing.